The Pinnarism Project

By

Peter Tyrer

This is a story about cats. Readers who wish to extrapolate to any other species can do so at their leisure.

impspired@gmail.com

Cover designed by Steve Cawte

ISBN: 978-1-915819-45-1

For Conor

OTHER TITLES BY IMPSPIRED

There is No Death in Finding Nemo –
by Jeffrey Feingold

Shrinking to Fit -
by John Eagles

Menopausal Mermaids & Life Lines –
by Sinead Coxhill

Honestly? It Never Bothered Me -
by John Doyle

Each Imaginary Arrow –
by Scott Ferry

Rueful –
by Kathleen Denizard

The Bones of the Story –
by Sandra Arnold

IMPSPIRED

GLOSSARY

Pinnarism: The belief that large-eared cats are inherently superior to small-eared cats

Anti-pinnarism (apinnarism): The belief that although all cats are equal it is necessary to promote the development and prospects of small-eared cats in order to counteract pinnarism

Posotism: The philosophy of promoting cats with small ears in favour of those with large ears so that pinnarism is reduced

Macropinnates: Cats with large ears

Micropinnates: Cats with small ears

HO's: Hearing Organs

CONTENTS

11 – Prologue May 20, C1020
15 - Chapter 1 Torpedo is dead.
19 - Chapter 2 A history lesson
28 - Chapter 3 Sagacity the Marmalade Cat.
34 - Chapter 4 Words have consequences
41 - Chapter 5 University Blues
51 - Chapter 6 School disturbance
57 - Chapter 7 Revising the Texts
64 - Chapter 8 At the Police Station
73 - Chapter 9 Felixtown Hospital
84 - Chapter 10 The Otic Revolutionary Guard
93 - Chapter 11 Orwell is arrested
99 - Chapter 12 Orwell on trial
112 - Chapter 13 Hamish is attacked
117 - Chapter 14 The Re-education of Orwell
131 - Chapter 15 The Secret Service arrests Hamish
135 - Chapter 16 Hut 8
137 - Chapter 17 The Amnesty
143 - Chapter 18 The Pinnarism Commission Writes a Letter
146 - Chapter 19 Sagacity explains
156 - Epilogue 23rd May, C1013

Prologue: May 20, C1020

'It is a fine May morning here in Downcat Street. We at the BBC, and indeed the whole cat community, are waiting for the Prime Minister and Mayor of Felixtown, Wilberforce Shorthair, to come out from Number 10 and address the nation. He now has a massive majority of 149, greater than any other government before him. We, and all in the four counties, are waiting in great anticipation.'

The cat flap opened at Number 10. The whispering and muttering of the crowd was silenced. Wilberforce came out and after two bounds jumped up five feet to the lectern and waved a paw to the crowd. A chorus of mews rang down Downcat Street and far beyond.

'Good morning, cats of our four counties. I am glad we have a fine day to introduce what I hope will be an equally fine government. You have put your trust in me, and my party, and I hope we will not let you down. We have many problems to deal with, a serious debt crisis, a plague of rats, low fertility in many areas, and the continuing irritating presence of dogs. There is also gross cat inequality across the nation. I understand your feelings of despair that so much good feline talent is being squandered. But we will not allow this to continue'.

An even louder chorus of yowls and mews rang out in appreciation.

'But before we address these problems we have another that is much more important, the most important since our Silent Revolution of 1,000 years ago when we took over the human race. They thought we were their pets; little did they know they had become our servants. The bigger challenge lies ahead. I know that you have elected me because we have promised to eliminate pinnarism. This is the real plague affecting our society. For centuries we long-eared macropinnate cats have dominated society. The tide has now turned. We will no longer allow those with big ears to take control as though it was their right; we will give the micropinnates their proper due after centuries of discrimination, and we will ensure that pinnary balance is to be placed at the heart of our nation's policies.

For far too long we have embraced the fiction that those with small ears are not only unable to hear everything that is said but are inferior in many other ways.'

He raised his voice and spoke carefully and deliberately.

'We now know this to be false. It is the invidious cause of stigma that must be eliminated from society. We must accept that many micropinnates are superior to the rest of us in their thinking, understanding, and intellect.'

"Down with big ears", yowled a micropinnate from the crowd.

'I understand your feelings, sir. But this is not the way forward. We have to embrace all cats as equal in society. I need to remind you of the wording of the First Amendment of our blessed Feline Constitution, that "all cats are created equal and are possessed with certain unalienable rights, and that amongst these are life, liberty, hunting and the pursuit of curled-up sleepfulness". Equality and diversity are our watchwords. We must never be prejudiced against any other cat because of the magnitude of their ears. We need to overhaul the centuries-old thinking that has led to systemic pinnarism in society and a root and branch reform is going to be necessary. 'Tough on pinnarism, and tough on the causes of pinnarism' has to be our new slogan. I hope that you, together with all the anti-pinnarist forces that I know lie behind our massive election victory, can join with me in ensuring that by abolishing pinnarism for good we can change the lives of everyone in this glorious nation.'

Wilberforce jumped down and was back through the cat flap into 10 Downcat Street in an instant. There was a short pause, followed by a cacophony of cat applause in every possible musical key, including some of such height and depth that it would be impossible for the Cat Laureate, Andrew Lloyd Webfoot, to reproduce them in a musical score. A new era had begun. Pinnarism was dead and would no longer be tolerated in cat society.

CHAPTER 1 Torpedo is dead

Hamish rushed into the kitchen.

'Mum. Its Torpedo. He's not well'.

She ran outside. Torpedo lay stretched out by the hedge. He loved stretching. But something was wrong. His fur was matted, his legs were all wrong and his tail was still.

She muzzled up to him and licked his chin. He did not move. Then she saw it.

'He's dead, Hamish. Look at his neck. He's been bitten. Look at his throat'.

Hamish looked. Yes, there was a red line just below Torpedo's chin with congealed blood just below. And he was certainly dead. If he was alive, Torpedo would never have allowed such a close examination of his neck without giving you a nasty nip. He was a very private cat.

Hamish stared into the distance but, like all cats, did not cry. But he was very upset.

'Who do you think did this, Mum?'

'I think it's pinnarism, Hamish'.

'What's pinnarísm?'

'It's a long story, Hamish. You must have been aware that Torpedo has smaller ears than you. There has long been an idea, a ridiculous idea, that cats with small ears are not as good as those with bigger ears like you. So those with small ears are looked down upon and hated by some cats with big ears.'

'But that's completely stupid. Where did that idea come from?'

'It's a long and complicated story and I only know a bit about it. When all the cats came into our district after the big Fen floods over 300 years ago there was trouble. Many cats did not like the new arrivals and tried to get them to leave. Then it was noticed that many of visitors had smaller ears and then pinnarism developed.'

'Pinnarism. That's a stupid word, what does it mean?'

'The posh word for an ear is a pinna, Hamish. So the annoyance and anger that the cats felt for these small-eared cats had to be made into a new word. Pinnarism is simply prejudice against cats with small ears. It's as stupid as saying that cats with white whiskers are better than other cats, as we all know cats' whiskers come in lots of different shades, but there it is'.

Hamish was both distressed and annoyed. He ran over into the corner of the garden and then galloped back to the pole by the kitchen door. He jumped up and stuck like a burdock on the pole for a short time. This was a good place for a cat to think. You had to concentrate so going off to sleep, always a desirable alternative, was not possible. Then, after the deep thought that only comes to cats occasionally, he made a decision.

'Mum, I am going to know more about pinnarism. My plan is to go round Felixtown and ask questions, not just to friends, but everybody. I am just an ordinary cat and they won't mind me asking. I think it would help me understand about Torpedo and whether pinnarism was the cause of his death.'

'All right, Hamish. But you must be careful. I've heard that even the most innocent of questions about pinnarism can get people into trouble. I'd also like to know the answers too. But take Orwell with you as well. I don't want him to see Torpedo like this – it will upset him. I'll get it all sorted out by the time you come back. It's all very upsetting; Torpedo was such a gentle cat, why should anybody want to kill him?' Mum was distracted, she could not take everything in, even though she was a very well organised cat who had firm resolve.

Hamish agreed, a little reluctantly. Orwell was a good cat to be with, always lively, always interesting, but too often he spoke without thinking, or, even if he did think, he liked to create a stir and often said much more than he should. The trouble with him was that he loved attention. When he was a kitten he just loved being surrounded by other kittens when he attempted the Ball Roll Feat, a competition for kittens to stay perched on a ball as it rolled down a special slope. Very few kittens ever completed it, but Orwell never stopped trying as he loved being in the limelight. He fell off and was bruised so many times he was called Sorewell, but that only made him even more determined.

'Who knows most about pinnarism, Mum? We need to go to the experts first'.

'The two wisest cats in Felixtown are Old Dunstable and Sagacity. You must see them first. But please make sure you come back for tea. It will be a sad tea without Torpedo. We must not forget him.'

Chapter 2 A history lesson

It was not easy to forget about Torpedo's death. He was a cat who could run twice as fast as any other member of the family so his brothers were convinced he had not been outrun; he had been ambushed. They trotted outside their hut carefully. There was little to see that was strange but as they moved away from home Orwell noticed a crumpled badge by an elder bush. It had the initials SS written on it.

'SS, what does that mean? It's just a hiss noise, just a warning', Orwell concluded.

They continued on their way. Following Mum's advice, Hamish and Orwell decided to call first on Old Dunstable, the grand old cat who knew feline history better than all other cats. Stories about him were told all around the town. Nobody knew how old he was. He must have been at least 25, but his knowledge of cat history went back for hundreds of years. He was noted for an amazing memory; put down by other cats to his unusual diet. He fed on cod roe every day, maintaining this opened up every corner of his mind, 'shines the windows to my soul', he called it. He was always ready to give his knowledge to visitors and so welcomed Hamish and Oscar with enthusiasm. History teaching for young cats was one of his favourite subjects.

'Thank you for your time, Old Dunstable. Our Mum thinks, and we agree, that you can help us to understand something we don't', said Hamish, who always tried to come straight to the point'.

'It's about ears', added Oscar, even more to the point.

'Ah, the sensitive subject of ears. I take it you wish to know more about pinnarism?'

'Yes, Orwell, he's my brother, and I, both want to know when it all started as our other brother, Torpedo, has just been killed by somebody and we think that this is because he has short ears'.

'I am so sorry to hear that, but these killings still continue. Unfortunately, every unexpected death is now thought to be connected to pinnarism so it is blamed for everything. It may or may not be true, but it is making everybody very nervous. When the government attacks pinnarism there is always a reaction from pinnarists.

All this may seem to make very little sense to you if you have not come across pinnarism before. But I can see you have had a nasty shock with the death of your brother so you had better come in and have a little cream. It always lifts the cat spirit'.

Hamish and Orwell joined him in a thick bowl of cream, which delighted them, and after a few laps, as they did not want to be greedy, sat at the edge of his big woolly speckled rug.

'It all started well over 300 years ago', Old Dunstable said with a sigh, 'a time nobody else remembers apart from me, when large numbers of cats came into our neighbourhood. They were fleeing from the fens, land which lies very low and which was completely covered by flood water. So, the cats had to come west and thousands came here. There wasn't enough food for them and they were asked to move on. But there was really nowhere to go to, and wherever they went they were unwelcome. The ones who were allowed to stay were given all the tasks that nobody else wanted, emptying litter trays, looking after dying cats in care homes, and sentry duties to keep dogs away.'

'So, they became your slaves', said Orwell.

'Shhh, you mustn't say that word', said Old Dunstable, flashing a long white paw in Orwell's direction. "Slaves" is not in the cat dictionary. As you know, all cats are allowed their independence, and no cat can have their lives controlled by any other cat.'

'Sorry', said Orwell, not really sorry. "Slaves" was staying in his dictionary.

'After a little while,' continued Old Dunstable, 'it was noticed by many of the other cats that the new arrivals tended to have smaller or shorter ears. So 'small ears' soon joined up as 'smears' and before long, when anyone wanted anything done, and felt it was beneath him or her, they shouted 'come here, smears'. All this was a little unfair but it set the tone. The new arrivals tended to have less food to eat, they acted as servants (not slaves remember) and as they all stayed together and interbred their ears also got even smaller.

Matters became so bad that the 'smear cats' were forced into corners where they lived completely separate lives – no wonder some called it cat-apart-hide – and met the big-eared cats rarely, and then only as servants. This became a serious matter of concern at the highest levels of government, not least as the smaller-eared cats were gradually being excluded from society and not contributing to our prosperity. So, the government had to act. It recommended that all prejudice against small eared cats should stop. The act of abusing, exploiting or making fun of small-eared cats was defined as pinnarism. But that hasn't stopped the prejudice. Adding the new word just gave added attention to ears.

It was established by our cat scientists that small eared cats generally do much less well in life than long-eared cats. They live shorter lives, get more diseases and do not earn as much as their long-eared relatives. So, the call came out to the cat community. Stamp out pinnarism altogether; it is a scourge.'

'So, is it working?' asked Orwell. 'The cats with small ears at our school don't do well. Everyone says they're a bit dim; are they right?'

'No. That's precisely the problem, and you must be very careful with your language as you are showing evidence of pinnarism', interrupted Old Dunstable. 'Just imagine, if you got ignored by the teachers and they paid more attention to the other pupils with different ears, do you think you could learn just as well?'

Hamish agreed. But he wanted questions answered as well as asked.

'Is the plan working? It sounds as though it should be. Do small eared cats have better lives now than in the past? '

'I honestly do not know the full answer, but their lives have certainly improved. Everybody seems to think that pinnarism can be stamped out with these new rules but you can't change prejudice very easily. Even when a cat such as Socrates Silkywhite impresses everybody with his knowledge and reminding all that he has small ears, some say that he has copied all his ideas from cats with big ears and so is a fraud. He is not, he is a cat of very high standing, but we have many in society who prefer to believe in lies when they are more comfortable than the truth. Everybody knows that pinnarism is a menace in cat society but it's easy on the brain and gives simple answers to complicated questions. History doesn't help. Cats don't forget, and the stories about what happened when the fens were flooded and all the smaller cats came into this neighbourhood still dominate people's minds. They still call it The Invasion.

'So have big-eared cats always been the bosses?' asked Orwell, never one to mince his language.

'Oddly enough, not at all. Even longer ago, so much so it could be fable rather than fact, the cats living in this area were all small-eared cats. But then the big-eared ones invaded from the south and took all their lands. This was recorded in the Domesday Tract, a very long sheet of parchment of which only bits remain in museums, and this showed that nine tenths of all the land was transferred from small-eared cats to the big-eared ones. So, you could say the true owners of Felixtown are the micropinnates.'

'What's the answer, then', said Orwell. 'If we say quits are quits, stop all the arguments, say ear size doesn't matter anymore, and correct all the things that are making small eared cats annoyed, then we will all be happy.'

'We have already thought of that', said Old Dunstable gloomily. 'Correcting pinnarist inequality is often called 'reverse pinnarism', or 'anti-pinnarism', which favours cats with short ears. I know it sounds to be a good idea but it doesn't work. It does not take long for large-eared cats to smell a mouse as we say, and then many say that these cats have only got their positions because of their small ears. This is now described as 'posotism', or positive ear discrimination, and makes a lot of large-eared cats very angry. There is even a Posotism Brigade, an angry army of small-eared cats that goes around chanting the slogan; "Pinnarism is dead, the micropinnates will inherit the earth". That is not the answer. Cats have to be promoted on merit and any suggestion that someone gets promotion because of their ear size completely changes the picture. And then of course there is the danger of doubt. If small eared cats who are promoted are criticised that their selection is just based on their ear size, they lose confidence in their abilities, become less competent and other cats turn on them and say their promotion is unfair. So posotism is not the way forward.

But we do have the six modified cat commandments that Wilberforce Shorthair has asked every cat to be taught:

All cats are created equal

All cats ears and eyes are special

All cats are promoted on merit

All cats will be fair to each other and respect their diversity

All cats will honour their heritage

All cats will fight pinnarism

The first five are already well known but the last is not. How we follow the sixth commandment will determine the future and whether pinnarism can be defeated. But the fight does not have a clear way to proceed. If we go at it in the wrong way we will get the kind of reaction that led to the death of your brother. We need to be more subtle, to show all cats that pinnarism has created much heat but very little light, and is really of no value to any cat apart from a small minority whose only aim is to cause trouble. I call these, privately of course, the badalleycats who just love the sounds of chaos and confusion.'

Hamish and Orwell felt a warm glow of feeling towards Old Dunstable. He had talked to them as though they were grown-up and wise, even though they knew they weren't, had been quite open about difficult problems, and appreciated he had been very well-informed. They rose from the mat and crouched in front of Old Dunstable to rub noses.

Hamish then rose and made a thank you speech. Old Dunstable certainly deserved one.

'Mum said you would be very helpful, but when we tell her how helpful she will be quite amazed. We have learnt much and hope we will forget little of what you have said'.

Old Dunstable was clearly pleased.

'Thank you both. May I wish you all the best in your travels and don't forget to come back when you have finished. I am always learning and am sure you will come across new ideas and suggestions. Please come back when you have ended your journeys and tell me what is new. I am not optimistic about the future at present but am very willing to change my mind. You can't teach an old cat new tricks but you can trick an old cat into thinking again. But remember some of what I have told you is very sensitive and it would be best if you did not mention my name in this context. I have to keep a balance between the pinnarists and posotists and this is not easy.'

Chapter 3. Sagacity the Marmalade Cat

Hamish and Orwell followed the hedge to the house on the hill where Sagacity lived. They were interrupted by a set of piercing yowls, followed by a crowd of small-eared cats who ambushed them on both sides of the path.

They started to chant,

'Small ears good, big ears bad' in the stretched out jeering tone only cats can produce without ever taking a breath, ending with a high-pitched whine.

'Ignore them', Hamish muttered to Orwell.

But Orwell would not ignore them, that was not his style.

He turned round and stared at their leader,

'You're just smears, we've no fears', he chanted back at them.

'Stop it', said Hamish. 'You're a pinnarist if you say things like that. They're just trying to get their own back after being trodden on for so long'.

After a short stand off during which all the cats stood and stared, the chanting stopped and they climbed up the hill. The words 'Let Wisdom Guide' was etched into the gate at the entrance to Sagacity's house, A large marmalade cat was sitting on his front paws staring at them from the porch.

'Can I help you? I don't think we've met before'.

'No. Old Dunstable suggested we came for advice about pinnarism as only you understand it properly'.

'And can tell us how to stop it', added Orwell unnecessarily.

'Well, that was very generous of Old Dunstable, but I don't think I fully understand it either and certainly don't know how to stop it. It seems very clear at first but the more you explore the more complicated it gets. But you had better come in and have a sip of my special cream before I explain'.

'The simple explanation of pinnarism is absence of respect. ' Sagacity paused as he swatted a fly that had come too close to the bowl of cream. 'Cats with small ears have been disrespected for generations. They have been looked down upon, taken for granted, verbally and physically abused, and barred from all the important jobs such as teaching to hunt, standing up to dogs and tree climbing. There is no good reason for this unfair treatment; it is a consequence of prejudice, pure and simple.'

'But small eared cats are a bit stupid, aren't they, just a bit', interrupted Orwell.

'Shush, don't say that word'.

Hamish wished Orwell would moderate his language; he was completely thoughtless.

'No', said Sagacity severely. 'Most certainly not. Let me tell you why. If you had been deprived of education, apart of course from that provided by your mother, who couldn't care less about the size of your ears, you would appear stupid too. But for years we have not given small-eared cats the chance to grow and thrive. As a consequence, they think, or more accurately used to think, as matters are improving, they are less able than others, and so many do not bother to compete with long-eared cats. We cats call this state of mind '*onoclor*', as when small eared cats submit easily to others they forget they have claws that are just as powerful as those of other cats. So, when *onoclor* affects everybody these poor renegades remain second class cats, felines that never expect to be any different until the day that the Cat on High calls them at the time of their passing.'

'So, we have to change'. Hamish asked the obvious question.

'Yes, we certainly do', said Sagacity. 'And have a few crunchy biscuits before I continue, as now we are now coming to the difficult bit. What we need to do is to give every small-eared cat the same chances in life that we currently offer large-eared ones, and also recognise their diversity. That's not easy, as although we are told all cats are equal, they come in many different shapes and sizes and cannot be completely equal, no matter what the cat commandment says. Some cats are better at running, some better at climbing, some better at hunting, so in that sense they are not equal. What equality means here is that we give all cats the chance to do the best they can with their natural talents.'

'That's easy', said Orwell without thought. 'When it comes to ears, all these are the same. The ears don't matter'.

' Yes, of course they don't, but you can't change attitudes overnight. We long-eared cats have grown up believing we are superior and it will take more than a few well-chosen mews to change this viewpoint'.

'Old Dunstable has told us much about the history of pinnarism', said Hamish, 'and he was clear that it would not disappear easily, but are we winning the argument? Is pinnarism getting less?'

'I honestly do not know. It puzzles me greatly. Since we've made people more aware of pinnarism it seems to have become more frequent, but of course this may be that it is getting identified more easily yet at the same time getting less. I think you young cats with your noses to the ground can help a great deal here. What you need to do is to visit all the important groups in Felixtown; the schools, the university, the police station, the hospital, the library, and ask your questions there. You have the advantage of being young and innocent, so you can ask questions that older cats would be afraid to ask. Everybody is now afraid of being labelled as pinnarist and many have stopped asking the right questions. You can break through that, but you have to be careful'.

Hamish and Orwell realised it was time to go home. They thanked Sagacity with special nose rubs and left through the Wisdom gate.

Mum was pleased to see them back.

'I hope you learned a lot about this stupid pinnarism. Are you now clear what it's all about?'

'Not exactly'. Hamish was careful in his reply.

'We have learnt what it is, how it started and developed, and what is being done to get rid of it. But the last part is the most difficult. We thought today we would understand why pinnarism was so harmful and have an easy explanation for why Torpedo was killed. But we didn't get it. Sagacity has given us a job to do, he is asking us to be detectives and investigators and we will have to plan our moves carefully. It is going to take some time'.

Mum was impressed.

'My o my. You have grown up fast. I always said you

were a serious boy at heart. Keep at it, and hope you can find justice for Torpedo. He didn't deserve to die like that'.

Chapter 4 Words have consequences

Hamish and Orwell had taken a few weeks to organise their visits to all the places Sagacity had noted down for them. Still, they had continued to talk to any cats in the town prepared to talk about pinnarism; they were still learning and wanted to examine all sides of the subject. Like all cats they were highly perceptive to other cats' behaviour. But they began to notice their conversations were getting more difficult. Many cats wanted to avoid talking about pinnarism. They wrinkled their noses and immediately changed the subject to mice, a subject everyone could agree on. One put it bluntly to Orwell, 'we don't do pinnarism. You talking about it makes you a pinnarist'. Attitudes were changing, and not always in the right direction for their enquiries.

They hoped, with summer coming, that people would become more open when they asked their questions. Mum gave them her advice. 'Wait a little. Cats deal with problems in their own time. You cannot rush them'.

But one morning there was a new development. A letter, quite a heavy one, clunked as it came through the cat-hole and hit the floor. Mum went over and picked it up in her teeth.

'It's addressed to you, Hamish, and it looks official. I hope it's not serious.'

Hamish slit it open with one movement of his left paw. The words were in large letters:

'Dear Hamish.

I work for the Pinnarism Employee Relations Team (PERT) and have noted that in your journeys to different places in Felixtown you have been using a word that is now considered pinnarist. I refer to the word 'ears'. At a recent meeting of the Town Council a resolution was passed. The words of the resolution are below:

'From the 1st June the word 'ear' will no longer be used in cat communication. It is now to be included in the list of words that are considered pinnarist. Please note that, whenever reference is made to this subject, cats must either use the word hearing organs or, preferably, the initials 'HO'. As a group, those with small hearing organs can be described as micropinnates and those with larger ones, macropinnates.

I hope you will note this in your future conversations. It you wish to discuss this further we at PERT will be very happy to advise you. The sanctions to be applied to those who use the offending word have not yet been decided but they are likely to be severe'.

Yours whiskerly,

M Olotov, Language consultant (PERT trained)

Mum looked up anxiously.

'Is it serious?'

Hamish scratched his head, passing his paw across his right ear which became inverted.

'It's just the latest in the pinnarist story. We cannot use the word 'ear' any more. '

'That's not difficult then. Following that advice is not going to cause any trouble – but it is a useful word'.

Orwell appeared. He was sparring with a spider swinging from the ceiling on a thread but stopped after overhearing the conversation.

'What's this about ears? Have we stopped hearing now?'

'Don't get excited', scolded Mum. 'It's just part of the pinnarism project. We'll all be much happier when its finished'.

Orwell padded over to read the letter.

'This is just stupid. No wonder you've got your ear inside out, Hamish. You don't want to hear this. Pinnarism is out of control. If this goes on we'll have to stop using language altogether and go back to the old system of miaows, which we all know was pretty useless and often dangerous. Remember when I was a kitten floating on a log down a stream and you miaowed 'jump' and I thought your mew said 'don't', so I just sat there until mum dragged me off in her teeth before the stream reached the river. Well, that's going to happen again if we are going to get rid of common words like 'ears'.

What's next for the list? We'll have to abolish "listen" as you can't hear without ears and the word controllers will make out the word are pinnarist. And what will happen when deaf cats are having their hearing tested at these new 'HO Centres'. Will there be hidden microphones picking up any cat who uses the word 'ear' to talk about a subject that can't be described in any other way? You can't take this nonsense lying down. Unsheath your claws'.

Mum wanted to calm everyone down.

'It's only a change in language. it doesn't really matter. It goes on all the time. In any case, I quite like the term HO's; I wonder if we should write it in capitals or lower letters. Look, you've been working very hard recently. Why not take the afternoon and evening off and go and see that play by William Showshoe, *Felix the Burman,* it's had very good reviews. It's all about the famous general, Julius Felix, and nobody can remember what his ears were like.'

Hamish agreed. 'We need a break. It will be good to get pinnarism out of our minds for a bit'.

Oscar agreed, very reluctantly, as his anger was still boiling away.

In the evening when they were more settled they made their way to the Palace Theatre, jumping on walls and playing hide and seek in the hedges as they moved down High Tail Boulevard. They were looking forward to the play as it would be a rest from pinnarism, a subject that was beginning to rule their lives.

The play opened and the two cats were quickly absorbed in the plot. They joined the boos when Julius's friend, Brutepuss, was persuaded to be part of the assassination of Julius, and soon were adding to the pervasive rustling sound of the audience's claws treading the seats of the theatre in excited anticipation when Mark Abyssinianus, played by that great actor, Laurence Orlando, stood over Julius' dead body and cried out:

'O, pardon me, thou bleeding piece of earth,
That I am meek and gentle with these butcher cats'.

Hamish and Orwell were now deeply involved in the power of the play. Mark continued,

'Persians, Birmans, town and country cats, lend me your ears;
I come to bury Julius, not to praise him.
The evil that cats do lives after them;

The good is oft interred with their bones;
So let it be with Julius; let him lie, and muse about
all those killings in the park of Gaul and
whether their deaths were just and wise'.

Suddenly there was a loud whistle and four police cats rushed on to the stage. They dragged Laurence off the stage and shackled his paws with pelvic bone handcuffs.

'What are you doing that for?', mewed Hamish loudly.

'Didn't your HO's notice?', shouted the lead officer. 'You must have picked up the organs that he asked to lend. We warned him, but he said William Snowshoe's words could never be changed. He wouldn't listen, silly cat, and he'll now go down a long time for that offence'.

'But this famous play was written long before pinnarism was thought of'.

'The past is the past. But pinnarism is now, and some words are deadly. We cannot make allowances for the past. Rules are for now, so stop your nonsense, or I'll take you in for questioning'.

The play was rudely ended. The audience slowly left, grumbling about government interference and killjoy thinking, but afraid to make any open complaint in case they too were arrested.

Orwell was as incensed as earlier in the day.

'I told you pinnarism was out of control. We've got to do something about it before it destroys all our lives'.

Hamish could not disagree. What had started out to be a search for the killers of Torpedo had become a social revolution.

Chapter 5 University Blues

It was good that the next visit Hamish and Orwell had planned was to be at the highest seat of learning in Felixtown, the University of Catbridge. Sagacity had already given them an introduction to meet the Vice-Chancellor, Professor Raggaty Doll, in which he had included the words, 'they are earnest to know'. Orwell, of course, could not help repeating this as 'ear-nest to know, ear-nest to know, who's going to arrest me?'.

They trotted down the walkway to the Vice-Chancellor's office and were let in by a kitten undergraduate. She had a message strapped to her chest 'No Pinnarism at Catbridge'.

'That makes the position clear', said Orwell. 'But why bother to tell the world something we are all meant to know and support'.

Raggaty greeted them at the entrance to his office. He gave Hamish and Orwell a quick sniff and asked them to lie down.

'Sagacity said you were doing a study on pinnarism. I was pleased to hear that. We need a bit more science to be attached to the subject. Can I ask you if you have any burning questions at this point so I can get my answers sorted in proper order?'

He turned briefly to pick up and crunch a mouse biscuit.

Hamish was prepared for this opportunity.

'We have been told by Sagacity about the history of pinnarism; how the cats with small HO's were treated as slaves and both despised and exploited by those with big HO's. How is this history being taught at the University of Catbridge and are there any lessons we should learn from this?'

'Yes', said Orwell, wanting to make it clear. 'If pinnarism ruled the world for so long do how do we explain its history in a way that is fair to everybody?'

Raggaty smiled, his whiskers appeared to fracture his face into lots of little triangles.

'Yes, you have done your homework. This was the subject of my PhD many years ago, "Pinnarism, past, present and future; what have we learned?". Many years ago, both at the time of the Domesday Tract and during the Cat Expansion Period, big HO cats colonised many parts of the world and introduced pinnarist principles to more primitive cat societies. This was not right or fair but I have to admit it was economically successful at the time even though we often deny it. So here at home we all benefited. We received more resources from the colonies, improved our standard of living and continued to exploit micropinnates. As these cats had only a little spare time in their lives they used it mainly to procreate. This led to many more micropinnates being born than macropinnates, further lowering their expectations in life and leading to more exploitation, all of which encouraged the pinnarists. It really made them feel they had created a just and fair society. But of course, it was all built on exploitation'.

'Is this why they now want to melt down the wax statues of colonising cats?' Hamish wanted answers quickly.

'Yes, indeed', Raggaty clearly approved of their homework. 'But here we have a problem, one that I developed this in my own thesis. It brings up the question, 'if pinnarism was successful in the distant past and led to prosperity should it be condemned today?' In absolute terms pinnarism is always wrong but should this mean we should rewrite the past? Some pinnarists were valiant, progressive and successful cats who added much to cat society – just remember the Oriental Shorthairs who introduced the mass importation of scratch posts from the Far East – so should we despise them for being pinnarists or praise them for their enterprise? The young cats of today have no doubts. In their minds all pinnarism is evil and always has been, so all past pinnarists should be judged in the same way as present pinnarists. So this is why they want to melt down all the statues'.

Orwell was fascinated, but wanted to take this further.

'So, if pinnarism is now hated and rejected, in all society and over all times. isn't there a risk that cats with large ears will now become hated by all?'

'Absolutely right', said Raggaty, looking quickly around him to make sure they were not being overheard. 'After centuries of pinnarism it is hardly surprising that small HO cats want to get their own back. Many of them want to take over cat society so they can dominate cats with large HO's and make them suffer for the evils of the past. This explains the growth of posotism. Revenge is a natural cat reaction; as you know, we cats are not known to be forgiving of others, ask the nearest mouse. There is a move to add another clause to the famous 'all cats are equal' manifesto, 'all cats are equal and none above the law'.

'What's wrong with that?', asked Hamish.

'Yes, it sounds innocent', agreed Raggaty. 'But the law of equality is being applied across the history of catkind. It did not exist in the past. So past inequality, even when it led to benefit, is now being exposed as both wrong and dangerous. This is a big problem for us in seats of higher learning. One of our best lecturers, Rosalind Devonfield, has been forced to resign over her series of lectures about Rum Tum Lugger, the captain of the notorious slave convoys that were brought over here from Europe 200 years ago. The students boycotted the lectures and said she was pinnarist, refusing to go to any more university teaching until she was dismissed. They said that as pinnarism was fundamentally wrong any lectures from the past that gave comfort, in any way, to pinnarism were also wrong, and probably unlawful. She tried to defend herself, saying she was only a historian describing the past as accurately as possible but it was no use. When we tried to support her we too were described as pinnarist so we just had to accept we were not going to win.'

'But that's not fair', Orwell interrupted. 'Straight talking is not a crime, cheating about the past is much worse'.

'Of course it's not fair'. Raggaty was now getting emotional. 'But cat society at present is not interested in fairness, only accountability. The thing we fear most is our university being labelled as institutionally pinnarist. It would drastically reduce our student intake and there would be demonstrations against us everywhere.'

Hamish was puzzled.

'But how can a place like a university be labelled as pinnarist? It's a building going back many years and so it can be called institutionally educational as teaching is at the core of your work, but pinnarism is not connected at all. If a few wild cats make pinnarist statements they can be called pinnarist but that cannot be applied to the university.'

'Unfortunately, that is precisely the problem', Raggaty gloomily observed. 'As soon as these sillier cats are identifed as university students people jump to conclusions and say we teachers are responsible for their views. We can then punish, or even expel them from the university but the pinnarist label remains - it sticks like glue.'

Hamish took a short time to take all this in. Pinnarism was getting more and more complicated.

'But when Wilberforce Shorthair made his speech a few months ago he made it all sound so simple. 'Tough on pinnarism, tough on the causes of pinnarism', he said. We just had to change our views and be fair to everybody. What you have said makes it more like 'pinnarism is tough, the causes of pinnarism are tougher.'

Raggaty stood up and shook away a few golden hairs from the fur on his back; they gleamed in the sun as they floated gently to the floor.

'Yes, I agree. But being tough on the causes of pinnarism strikes a chord; it is a great slogan that, like all great slogans, means very little. The causes of pinnarism go back generations and they will not change pinnarist thinking overnight. We have to be both tolerant and patient. But some are not prepared to be patient and are determined to punish any cat that says anything that could be remotely seen as pinnarist. So, when Rosalind praised Rum Tum Lugger for his organisational skills in her lectures she was immediately branded a pinnarist, even though nobody could deny he was a great organiser and leader. No amount of fur flannel can take that away. Nowadays it is impossible to say anything positive about someone with a pinnarism present or past, as we have declared them all to be universally evil. The free mew has been suppressed by a hiss'.

'So, what can we do to make things better?', asked Hamish,

'It looks bad, but you are in a better position than most to change attitudes. I understand from Sagacity that your brother was almost certainly killed by a pinnarist group so you can't be faulted. What you must do is to tell your friends not to lose their sense of proportion, not just to react with vengeance when they come across pinnarism, not to assume that every case is motivated by prejudice, not to follow the mob. You must educate, educate, and educate, otherwise I fear our country will go backwards into oblivion and become a primitive society again. You could start with the schools. Once a kitten learns something important is stays for life. Go to the School Academy close by.'

He paused, picked a sheet of paper and scratched a message.

'Give this to Elena Titova, the headmistress, when you arrive at the Academy. She is in tune with me about pinnarism and is trying to change attitudes there. But please do not tell anyone that I have given you this advice. My position is now uncertain. Who knows if I will be next for abuse and dismissal and I no longer have the energy to fight. I am now well past my sell-by date as a superannuated professor and I want to spend the rest of my days in relative comfort.'

'Did you hear that, Orwell. No word to anyone about this. But you have given us our mission, Professor Doll. We can only overcome pinnarism by good sense, logic and reason. It is time for us to stretch our forepaws, unsheath our claws, and stiffen our tails for action. Thank you again, we hope to show you we have learned from your advice and if we can persuade every cat that he or she is at least as good as every other, then pinnarism, posotism and all the new words we would love to forget can be banished from catworld, as then they will no longer be necessary.'   Hamish stopped, as Orwell was giving him his 'stop being pompous' look.

'I can only wish you Cat Speed in your efforts', said Raggaty as he escorted them out of his office. The kitten undergraduate was surprised by this; escorting visitors was her task, so the interview must have been special.

As Orwell and Hamish were leaving the campus they saw a group of cats crowded around a small fire with a large pot close by.

'What's in there?', Orwell asked,

'That was Rum Tum Lugger, now just sludge', said a cat with small HO's proudly. 'That's the end of pinnarism on our campus. We're going to cast another one in the form of Nonbi to replace it'.

'Nonbi, I haven't heard that name before. Who's Nonbi?', asked Hamish.

'Nonbi Chinchillier, she's in line to be our new Prime Minister. The Scourge of Pinnarism they call her. She's tougher than Wilberforce and is bound to be elected'.

Orwell, always keen to deflate others, couldn't resist a jibe.

'And will they be melting her down in a hundred years' time'.

'Of course not. Why are you saying that and who do you think you are?'

'Times change. When Rum Tum's statue was cast 150 years ago they must have all applauded like you, but praise never lasts'.

Small ears was getting tetchy.

'Now you two clear off. You're aliens here. We don't want you stirring up trouble'.

Hamish and Orwell wheeled round and trotted away, not too fast and with their tails held high, showing that they were leaving on their terms. Their first go at education had not gone especially well but they were learning fast.

Chapter 6 School disturbance

Hamish and Orwell were reminded that Sagacity, like Raggaty, had suggested that after visiting the university it would be good to see how pinnarism was being approached at the younger end of the cat spectrum, kittens at school.

They had been helped by the note Raggaty had given them. It just said; 'Elena. This introduces Hamish and Orwell; they are students doing a survey on pinnarism. How schools teach this would be very helpful to them, so I hope you can welcome them.'

They climbed through the railings of Felixtown Primary Academy and found their way through to see the headmistress, Mrs Elena Titova, a Russian Blue. She was crisp, brisk and well organised. She looked at the note:

'Excellent, we have lots for you to learn about at this school. Pinnarism should not really be a problem here, unless it's brought in by the parents. But that's for you to find out. Perhaps one of you can go outside and talk to the kittens as its playtime now, and the other can stay with me.'

Orwell went out into the playground. Over in one corner there was a crowd of cats in a ring and lots of shouting. He rushed over to see two cats sparring on the ground, every so often stopping to stare at each other before jumping together again with unsheathed claws. The crowd around the circle were shouting. 'Watch his right paw, Moby', 'Don't turn your back on him', 'Spit in his face'. As those looking on were doing nothing Orwell jumped into the ring and separated the two kittens. They stood, rigid, staring balefully at each other.

'What's all this about?'. Orwell was determined to get to the bottom of this.

'He called me a smear', said the smaller of the two cats.

'So what? You've got small HO's, he's got long ones. You could have called him a lear – a cat with large HO's – and then you would have been even'.

'But "smear" is nasty, very nasty'. The small kitten was now almost in tears.

'Is only nasty if you make it so. And why did you say it?', said Orwell, turning towards the larger kitten.

'He was annoying me. He kept on pawing at my neck, said I needed a collar'.

'Is that a good reason for saying he was a smear?'

'No, but cats with small HO's are often like that'.

'So, what you are saying is that cats with small HO's

are more likely to paw the necks of other cats. Is that correct?'

The macropinnate kitten was embarrassed. 'No, not really'.

They all stood silently, including the crowd looking on.

Orwell felt it was time to introduce some education. That's what Raggaty would have wanted.

'Let's get this clear. You called him a smear because you knew it would upset him; no more, no less. But haven't you heard the expression I was taught by my mum, 'sticks and stones may break cat bones, but mews will never hurt me'? Now if you', said Orwell, turning to the smaller kitten, 'had just said nothing, or just called him a lear, this fight would never have happened. Whether we have small or large HO's has nothing to do with it. If you said "big nose" or "small nose" to each other instead of referring to HO's you wouldn't have got nearly so upset. So, the next time you have an argument don't involve HO's. You can pick on your noses, your tongues, your whiskers, your paws, it doesn't matter which, and then you won't get upset.'

'What about colour?', said a brightly variegated tabby in the ring of onlookers.

'You can always try that', laughed Orwell, 'but making fun of your colour would be ludicrous. You've all the colours of the rainbow on you, so there is no such thing as feline colour prejudice as we would all have it. Colour prejudice could never exist in cat society - it would make us dizzy'.

He turned to the two kittens, now exhausted after their fight.

'So, rub noses, save your energy and don't let your HO's prevent you from being friends. What's on top of your head is less important than what's inside'.

The bell rang for the end of playtime and the kittens all returned to the school.

Hamish had been talking to Mrs Titova in her office.

'Our advisors have suggested to us that pinnarism is not found very often in kittens. There seems no such thing as natural prejudice. Would you agree?'

'Yes, I certainly do.' But then she stopped and leaned forward to whisk a fleck of rust from Hamish's head. She was clearly a very particular headmistress.

'We have kittens of all types here at the Academy and in lots of colours and shapes. In general they get on very well, even those that come from less well-off homes. I always think that school is a great leveller. All kittens are nervous when they arrive but they quickly find a group of friends and when I go into the playground I find so many different groups of such variety. And HO's don't figure in the groups at all. Yesterday I was so proud to see the most diverse group of all, an Abyssinian, a Manx, a Bengal and a Bombay, all playing together at Chase the Marbles without a single cross mew between them. And I don't need to tell you the variation in HO's between them is enormous. So pinnarism is simply absent. It only comes about when parents pass their prejudices on to their children and pretend it is part of their education.'

'So how do you think we ought to deal with the problem. Do you retrain the kittens or deal with their parents'.

'Young man, you have much to learn', said Mrs Titova, laughing to show a set of exceptionally sharp white teeth. 'We would love to re-educate the parents but it would be a nightmare. Our job is to teach kittens the rudiments of education before they go off into the jungle of the feline workplace. Our teaching of pinnarism is very simple. We don't mention it our lessons unless it is brought up in discussion. When it is mentioned, we say this was an error of the past and is no longer present so there is no need to say anything more.'

Orwell padded in from the playground.

'Ah, young man, what have you been learning in the playground. You look quite pleased. I hope you were impressed by what you saw'.

'Yes and no, miss. There was a fight in the playground but I think I sorted it out'.

'Oh dear, a fight'. Mr Titova lifted a paw to obscure one eye, almost as though she did not want to know about this stain on the smooth running of her school.

'What was it all about?'

'One of the kittens said another was a smear, and so there was quite a nasty argument. I got them, and all the others watching, to agree to stop all comments about HO's and if they really wanted to be silly and to make fun of others to pick on other differences between them. I don't know if they will, but at least they were listening.'

Mrs Titova beamed so much her face seemed to be twice as large.

'That is quite excellent. You are a very clever kitten. I will remember this when pinnarism next comes up in discussion. 'Other organs in, HO's out', will be the message.'

'Well', she said rising to her feet and raising her tail high in approval, 'I must say it has been such a pleasant experience seeing you today. You have helped my education at least as much as your own. I suggest you next visit the library, where you will find all the staff hard at work removing the taint of pinnarism from all our books'.

Chapter 7. Revising the texts

Hamish and Orwell moved on to the library close to the school. Fortunately they arrived at the same time as a history lecture was about to be given to kittens visiting from one of the schools close by. A Tonkinese cat with large green eyes was giving the talk. The label in front of her desk read 'Mrs Min Doras works at Felixtown Library: Where Curiosity Lives and Smiles'.

Once she had understood the reason for their visit, Min was happy for Hamish and Orwell to sit in on the lecture.

'I know you are older kittens, but I am sure I will be able to tell you something new', she said, out-staring them with her green orbs.

Min had a firm penetrating voice.

'Behind me, kittens, are the books you need to read on colonial pinnarism. This is the subject of today's lecture. This is not an easy subject for kittens to understand so I must ask you to concentrate. Colonial pinnarism are two words that are not easy to remember, but if you think of the words 'being bad to foreigners' you can get the idea. The 'foreigners' as we judged them to be, 200 years ago, lived in wild parts of the world and in today's language we would have said they were uncivilised. Cats with large HO's were dominant in other countries and they ignored the wild ones outside and thought of these other cats as aliens. When they took over the rest of the cat kingdom instead of trying to understand these other cats they imposed their own language and habits without thought. As you probably all know, small HO cats like to groom each other by first licking behind the HO's before moving round to the top of the head. Cats with large HO's lick the top of the head immediately and do not move round to the HO's until much later. But the pinnarism that dominated the thinking of the colonising cats took over. All cats were taught to groom on the top of the head first. They were told it was more hygienic as there were fewer bugs on the head. But they were given no option and there is no scientific reason for this. So, when you hear about top-head grooming think of it as colonial pinnarism. It is stupid, arrogant and thoughtless. So we are now in the process of correcting all the books on the subject. All references to preferred head-grooming are being erased and it is now made clear in all our books that grooming in any order is perfectly acceptable and recognises the diversity of cats.'

Orwell had to interrupt.

'But you can't rub out things that have happened. What's wrong with saying things have changed'.

Min responded, very quickly. 'I will answer that question when this lecture is over. We must not confuse the other kittens'.

The lecture continued with frequent references to the way in which the large HO cats had exported all their scientific, hunting, and medical ideas, whether they were true or not, to the colonies, where they were taught as fact. Once this became established the culture and expression of these dominated regions was all but crushed. As Min put it, 'a whole history was wiped out and forgotten'. But fortunately, now, as a consequence of the pinnarism project they were being revived.

She was getting near the end of her talk. She held up a book with both front paws. 'Colonial Pinnarism Exposed'. In smaller type below was the author's name, 'Min Doras'.

'This is the book you must read to get the background to this lecture. It has been reviewed by the Felixtown Chronicle. They have been very kind to me and have summarised the book even better than I could have done myself, with the words, 'the book is for cats of all ages and breeds and we can now say it will be critically acclaimed in its field'.

Orwell heard this at the back of the room.

'Large cow pat' he muttered.

'What was that at the back there?'

'Large cow pat', repeated Oscar. 'That's critically acclaimed in the field but if only cows go there it means nothing'.

Min spat. A long sliver of gleaming liquid fell just short of Orwell.

'I definitely need to see you after the meeting. The lecture is now over'.

Min shepherded Hamish and Orwell into her office.

'You must excuse my brother', said Hamish quickly. 'He talks before he thinks'.

'So I see, but your behaviour is quite disgraceful – you almost sabotaged my very well-prepared talk. I feel I may have to report you'.

Hamish again felt he had to take over before Orwell became annoying again.

'Our problem in understanding your work is this. History tells us what has happened, and if it is accurate it cannot lie. We can quite understand why today's cats have to be taught about the errors of the past but is it necessary to remove the evidence in the way you are doing?'

Min smiled, but the smile still kept her lips downturned.

'I understand your point, but you are wrong in your assumptions. We are not changing history but simply leaving some bits out. By not including colonial pinnarist behaviour, or indeed any other pinnarist statements in our books, we are making sure that our readers do not pick up pinnarist notions that they might well do if the books remained as they are. Omission is commission, we are bringing our books up to date so that there is no confusion in the young minds we are trying to educate'.

Orwell tried a different tack.

'Pinnarism isn't just in books. It is everyday language. If you go around Felixtown market you hear pinnarist comments all the time. You can take it out of books but not out of language'.

'You like arguing, young cat, don't you. Of course you are right, but eliminating pinnarism is a gradual process. If pinnarist attitudes and behaviour are removed from all our books eventually, over the generations, they will disappear from language too. Come, let me show you some books which have been revised in the way we want'.

Hamish and Orwell followed Min into the main library. She stopped at a History and Geography marker in the first bookcase. She pulled out 'The Story of Catkind: From Its Beginning to Now'. She quickly flipped through the pages with an elegant claw.

'Here we have the early account of the Domesday Tract. We do not want to include the evidence that the large HO invaders stripped all the land from the small HO cats who lived in the area – that is, before it became Felixtown, of course. So here we have revised the text, 'as the new cats were now in control of the country, they took over most of the land from those who owned it previously'. We do not say anything about HO's at all, even though you could say it would support the posotist position if we did, as it was the cats with small HO's who were wronged.'

'Potholes', said Orwell.

'You have an odd way of raising issues; I find it rather annoying'.

Orwell explained. 'Filling in potholes on the history road makes the journey smoother but they were still there. You cannot pretend they never existed'.

'Yes, but are they relevant to history? Surely the important part is the road, not the little imperfections in it'.

Hamish was not satisfied either,

'History is meant to record what happened as accurately as possible. So in the future historians may want to look at the time we are in now from a completely different perspective. So they need a true record of what happened. Of course, a full record of cat history does not exist, there are too many gaps. But is there somewhere in Felixtown where the most accurate full history of the past is written?'

Min smiled.

'You have hit on a sensitive subject. Professor Raggaty Doll has a full record in the University archive but he is refusing to let us revise it. But we are working at it, and in the end we will wear him down.

I hope I have satisfied you with my answers. I suspect not, but you are still learning, and eventually you will see things from my point of view'.

Mrs Doras turned on her elegant back paws, tossed her tail high in the air, and strode off without a further word.

Chapter 8. At the Police Station

'That wasn't too good, was it, Orwell?', said Hamish as they passed out of the Library and down the road to the centre of Felixtown.

'They seem to have got a curious solution to pinnarism; pretend it never happened. Well, that can't possibly apply to the Police Station. Everyone is now saying it is institutionally pinnarist'.

Orwell stopped and looked at his brother. It was time to ask some serious questions.

'What does 'institution' mean?'

'I think it just refers to a place where people work or spend time together'.

'So, if two of our Marble Rolling Group of five kittens were pinnarist this would make the Marble Group institutionally pinnarist?'

'Not really, as your group isn't an institution. You only meet when you are rolling marbles'.

'Well then, that would mean if the people who run Felixtown Football Club were pinnarist, you could not say they were institutionally pinnarist as they only meet to play football.'

'No, that's not right. You don't get paid to play marble rolling; the players at the Football Club are paid, as it's their job. And we know it's classed as an institution. The Felixtown Cricket Club is being investigated for institutional pinnarism as we speak'.

'Good, that makes it clear. So, if we at the Marble Rolling Group were paid for rolling marbles we too could be called an institution?'

'You're twisting my words'.

'No, I'm not. I am just being logical. That's what Raggaty asked us to be.'

'I have to admit I don't know what institutional pinnarism is either. But as the police as a group have been described as pinnarist we might get the answers when we go into the Station.'

They sidled in through a side door.

'Yes', said the petite Singapura at the desk. 'What is your business?'

'We have been asked to give a report on pinnarism by Sagacity. Can we see the senior officer for a short meeting?'

'This is most irregular, but it so happens that the Commissioner of the Force, Bryn Voss, is waiting for a visitor and he has not yet arrived. So, if he agrees, you can have a few words with him'. She was being helpful. Orwell winked at her.

'Watch out, young man, don't stretch your luck'. Singapuras can be quite severe. Orwell dropped his gaze.

An imposing Norwegian Forest cat appeared through a flap. He radiated authority.

"I am Commissioner Voss. I understand you are doing research on pinnarism. It's an absolute scourge here, and if you can help, in any way, I will be really pleased'.

'Thank you, Commissioner. We are just young cats but hope we can be direct? We cannot understand the word "institutional pinnarism" and yet we know it is being said very often about the police force. What exactly does it mean and what makes it institutional?' Hamish certainly was going straight to the point.

Commander Voss cleared his throat. He wanted to give a precise answer.

'People use the word 'pinnarist' about an institution when they guess, suspect or know - any of these - the culture in the organisation is pinnarist. Does that make sense?'

'Yes, but what does that mean? How do you measure culture? Is it something you can define?'

Orwell wasn't going to be left out. 'If I was pinnarist and persuaded two of my friends in our Marble Rolling Group to be pinnarist would that be our culture?'

Commissioner Voss smiled.

'Not exactly, but when I was a kitten we got very worked up about marble rolling, especially the ones on the outer track that picked up speed at the end – marvellous, weren't they. But you have brought up an important point. Our politicians, who want to show how clever they are by using expressions we never think of, say a culture of pinnarism is like pepper in a casserole – no matter how little or any part of the casserole you eat you can always taste the pepper.'

'But you can't taste pinnarism'. Orwell was not impressed.

'Granted, it's not the same. But the claim is, even though I dispute it, that the Police Force in Felixtown has many cats, possibly dozens, who make pinnnaristic remarks, or otherwise make fun of, or discriminate against cats with small HO's and nobody contradicts them or tells them it is wrong. Once these comments are not only unchallenged but accepted, then many argue that the Police Force shows institutional pinnarism. If everybody around you is showing pinnarist prejudice then it becomes acceptable to accept and repeat it. They also say we are pinnarist because we arrest, or stop in the street, more small HO cats than big HO ones. But this is because cats with small HO's are more likely to break cat laws as they come from more deprived communities. I accept this could be a result of pinnarism but it could equally well be good policing'.

'How can you identify pinnarism and stop it then? That sounds very difficult'.

'Two ways. First, we've just got to select the right cats for the police force, ones who are not prejudiced. We are making progress but the Mayor is threatening to attach members of the Otic Revolutionary Guard to our station to ensure all pinnarist offenders are identified. I'm trying to resist it as pinnarism will then revert to private conversations, but it may not work. I don't want to have a police state starting inside a police station; I can't see that ending happily. Secondly, we have to mind our language. Last week one of our police sergeants caused a great deal of trouble by saying at a public meeting 'cats in Whisker Hollow commit more crimes than others in Felixtown'. Cries of "institutional pinnarism" rang out across the area'.

'But that's rubbish', interrupted Orwell. 'Everyone knows that statement is true'.

'Yes, but he did not say it in the right way. If he had described crime in Felixtown and pointed out the areas with high and low levels nobody could object; these data are all publicly available. But by referring to cats in Whisker Hollow he was pointing out who was committing the crimes and we all know small HO cats make up most of the population there. Nowadays everybody is obsessed by language that could be regarded as pinnarist, even when it is completely innocent, or even a slip of the tongue. Last week on of my officers said to a cat who was tormenting others in the town square, 'come away from there, brother, you can see you're causing trouble'.

'What's wrong with that'.

'Nothing really, but as there is a tendency to call small HO cats 'brother' or 'sister' the silly cat reacted and reported him for pinnarism; our officer has now been suspended and cannot work until the disciplinary committee has made a judgement on his case.'

Orwell shook his head disbelievingly.

'It's nonsense, isn't it. You have to counter it with propaganda of your own. If you made a big splash and said you would recruit your police officers with equal numbers of large HO and small HO cats you would have everything balanced. If you did that could you say institutional pinnarism was dead.'

'Yes, it's a good idea. But to counter pinnarism we have been asked by the Mayor to employ more cats with small HO's than large ones; our quota is now to recruit 60 small to 40 large. That is going to introduce resentment as most of our staff have large HO's and I think this new rule will increase pinnarism, as well as promoting posotism, and do not see it helping in any way'.

Hamish was distressed. 'It looks as though you can't win. Institutional pinnarism clearly doesn't exist; it is just wordplay on language that would only apply to an organisation that only consisted of pinnarists. I get the impression it should be called convolutional pinnarism, it twists everything we say. It seems as if you do your job properly and speak plainly there is always somebody who will claim you are pinnarist. If you then accept all their suggested changes you then fail to be good police-cats. It's a pity you can't be like the local schools; by not talking about pinnarism at all they seem to get by'.

Commissioner Voss sighed.

'There is no hope of that here. There are a group of people, mainly politicians, who make their living by tossing 'institutional pinnarism' into every meeting like a grenade. The grenade explodes, everyone gets very angry and all other business gets lost. Being tough on pinnarism means that we are no longer being tough on crime.'

He was interrupted by his slinking Singapura secretary. Orwell was fascinated by her movement.

'Your visitors are here, sir'.

Commander Voss rose.

'Much as I would like to continue this conversation, the Otic Revolutionary Guard must take precedence now. I just hope they are not going to restrict us even more. I hope I have helped you'.

Hamish and Orwell left through the back hatch.

'Poor Commander Voss', said Orwell. 'Whatever he does he's going to lose. I'm never going to think of becoming a police cat. I'd just be a target for the mob'.

Both cats were in a serious mood as they made their way out of the police station past the Singapura kitten. Oscar gave her a wink from his other eye. She ignored him. But as they went just about to leave the grounds of the Police Station Orwell saw something he recognized by a rubbish bin. It was a cap with a badge. He recognized the lettering – SC – exactly the same as the one close to where Torpedo was killed.

Orwell was very disturbed. Something at the Police Station was linked to Torpedo's death. Was this anything to do with Commander Voss? Orwell could not believe it was. But there was too much else going on. He must put this out of his mind. It was time to visit Felixtown Hospital.

Chapter 9 Felixtown Hospital

The hospital in Felixtown was the pride of them all. The advances of the last twenty years had crystallised in the opening of the glossy building that showed all the new confidence of feline society.

Hamish and Orwell entered the main cat flap and were directed to the Prevention of Illness Centre, not their preferred option, but a sign saying 'preventing illness saves money and is cheaper than cure' suggested why they should start there.

In an airy hall there were cats of all types sitting in front of screens looking serious and concerned. Orwell found this far too boring and went off on his own.

Hamish went over and looked at one of the screens. In bold type was written:

"Aging is a natural and unidirectional process common to all cats. This has been increasing rapidly all over the world in recent years and this may pose a risk for elderly felines who are unaware".

Hamish was amazed, both at the sentiments and the curious language.

'Well now, if you can prevent aging you will have done something no species has ever done. Are you really serious about it?'

An Oriental shorthair heard and came towards him. She was elegant but her stare was so powerful and threatening it made Hamish shudder. But she spoke quietly and he was reassured.

'Pleased to meet you, young man, my name is Dr Nessie Wang. You ask if we are serious? We most certainly are. The problem we are addressing goes to the heart of catdom. Cats live to an average of 14 years but many live a lot longer. Wisdom comes with age and we need more wise cats to advise us, rather than a surfeit of scatter-brained kittens. 14 years is too young to lose a cat; we need more older cats. We also have a serious problem that is linked to pinnarism. Micropinnates die an average of two years before macropinnates.'

'Is that due to pinnarism?'

'Like many such questions the answer to it is only partly true. They have more heart disease, more fatal accidents and see doctors less often than other cats, so their illnesses are diagnosed later, sometimes too late. Pinnarism may be related to the failure to go for advice and if we are to prevent illness we must have the trust and confidence of all cats in society. Calling the differences 'pinnarism' makes many people feel better but, in all honesty, it offers nothing of value – it is just a vague pointer indicating the right direction. But please keep this to yourself and do not say this too loudly; it upsets some cats'.

'That's my impression too', said Hamish. 'But how can we change attitudes and will they lead to cats living longer?'

'I'll give you an example. We all know that cats are very clean animals and look after their most prized gift, their fur. But, as you must also know, some of the fur is taken into the stomach and intestines. If it completely blocks the intestine the cat can die. This happens more commonly with cats who have small HO's, and these are more frequently brought into hospital for operation. We are not very good at these operations and about a quarter of the cats die prematurely. Over there', she said waving a manicured paw, 'we have a training course especially focused on small HO cats to try and prevent fur balls, but it is not an easy task'.

They padded down towards the end of the room where a sign 'Fur Cleaning Programme' was displayed. Orwell had already arrived and was taking a great interest in the process. Four young cats with small HO's were taking part in an exercise. They were walking between two rollers a short difference apart, each with many small spikes that removed excess dead fur. It was certainly working well; at the end of each row were large mounds of fur of all colours.

'Samantha, Charlie, Henry and Chloe are all being trained in this programme. You can see it is very effective in removing excess fur.'

She turned to the four cats.

'I hope you are all pleased with the programme and are enjoying yourselves. It is much better than having an operation'.

Three of the cats nodded and smiled, but Samantha, a tabby-white Persian, turned up her already turned-up nose and just grunted.

Orwell decided he must speak with Samantha, so when the others had moved on, he approached her.

'Can I ask you some questions? You've probably been asked them before but please excuse me if I repeat them'.

'Of course'. Samantha seemed surprised to be asked so nicely.

'You don't seem very pleased about the fur cleaning programme. The other cats seemed to like it'.

'It's pinnarism, pure and simple. It's all set up for cats with large HO's'.

'But from what I have heard, and I may have got this completely wrong, they say it's especially helpful for cats with small HO's so it will help you more than most others'.

'That's just an excuse. Its pinnarism. One of my friends has done a big survey. The system says the cleaning programme has been specially set up for micropinnates but she found that three-quarters of the cats who go through the programme are macropinnates. So, it's a lie. Its set up for cats with large HO's.'

This puzzled Orwell even more.

'Many think that micropinnates do not look after their fur in quite the same way as macropinnates and that's why the Fur Cleaning Programme has been set up? That must be an advantage to you'.

Samantha looked at him sharply – her claws emerged menacingly from her front paws – they were very long.

'Absolutely not. The Fur Cleaning Programme is just a distraction set up by the pinnarists to hide their prejudice. We've advised all cats with small HO's to refuse it'.

Orwell was now getting exasperated.

'That doesn't make any sort of sense. Can we go back to the beginning. Do you agree fur cleaning is useful as it stops cats from taking fur, and all other kinds of nasty things that stick to fur, into their bellies. Do you agree with that?'

'Yes, of course'.

'So, any fur cleaning arrangement that prevents fur being swallowed is good for your health?'

'Yes, but the Fur Cleaning Programme has been set up for macropinnates'.

'But isn't the answer to campaign for more cleaning centres in areas of your choosing, not to refuse fur cleaning on principle?'

Samantha now extended all her claws. She was getting quite annoyed.

'It's quite obvious you know nothing about the cultural requirements of small HO cats. We are not like you, we regard fur cleaning as a joint task within the family, not some impersonal process in a centre run by strangers. You pinnarists are all the same. You assume you know us but you don't. You have transferred all those prejudices from colonial times to us in Felixtown today.'

Orwell realised this conversation was going nowhere.

'Thanks, Samantha. I've learnt a lot and I do not want to get into arguments, so I'll be leaving now'.

He jumped up and ran off. Samantha looked disappointed. She was enjoying the discussion but if he couldn't deal with straight-talking that was his business.

Orwell returned to Dr Wang and Hamish, who were walking down the path towards the Mental Health Unit.

Dr Wang was now in full flow; she was both talking and walking more quickly and her tail was restlessly moving from side to side.

'We have a different problem in feline mental health. Antisocial cats with violent behaviour are more likely to have small HO's than large ones. We have known this for many years. Not surprisingly, this means that more of them are admitted to the Mental Health Unit under compulsion using Cat Protection Sections. Some people say this is a consequence of pinnarism. It could be, but as we know that micropinnates tend to be more violent that macropinnates, it could be just a consequence of that only, but then others say that pinnarism is the reason for the violence and that explains the figures.

But we have just completed a survey and found that the numbers of compulsory admissions under Cat

Protection Sections, usually because of violence, are almost exactly in the same proportion whether or not micropinnnates or macropinnates are in charge of, and arranging, the admissions. But this does not stop many cats saying that pinnarism is the real reason for the problem, and if pinnarism was removed violence in micropinnates would be less.'

Orwell had joined them and intervened.

'I've just been talking to Samantha in the Fur Cleaning Programme. She says we don't take enough notice of culture in cats with small HO's. Could that be the reason for the difference in violence?'

'You have hit that particular nail on the head, young man', said Dr Wang approvingly. 'If you come from an environment where violence is normal then you use the same approach in other environments where it is not normal. In those settings threats of violence do not work. So, what we really need to do is to change micropinnate culture so that it is more respectful. But similarly, we need to be respecting the different culture of micropinnates.

If pinnarism is entrenched then respect is absent on both sides and we just have anger and more violence – and I do not need to tell you how much of premature mortality is due to trauma inflicted by other cats. I have to admit I see no answer, but just repeating 'pinnarism' means nothing without change.'

Orwell sighed. 'Wouldn't the easiest solution be to have a team of plastic surgeons to extend the ears of all small-HO cats so that nobody could tell the difference?'

'Yes, indeed. Some very rich cats with small HO's have tried it, but they all look a bit odd and everybody can identify how they were born. So, we have to continue to encourage, persuade, and, in some cases, force all cats to behave and act in the same way towards each other and then pinnarism will slowly die. But I don't want you to feel downhearted; look around the hospital and see how everything else is improving'.

Orwell and Hamish were puzzled. Everywhere they went they saw the same picture; everyone was against pinnarism but nobody really knew how to get rid of it. It was like a bad smell that would not go away.

They decided to leave the hospital and go home to Mum for tea. As they passed down Lithesome Avenue they saw another crowd. There were five black shorthairs attacking a tabby white Persian,

'That's Samantha', Orwell shouted as he bounded over and separated them.

'What's going on here?'

Samantha was in tears.

'They pounced on me when I left the Fur Cleaning

Programme. They said it was a waste of time any machine cleaning my fur as I would always be scruffy'.

'Is that true?' Orwell asked the biggest of the five cats.

'Yes, cats like her are stopping us from getting our fur cleaned. They shouldn't be allowed in the place.'

Hamish recognized this other cat, Groubador Fernandez, a rough black shorthair who lived in their neighbourhood and who was recognized as a bully.

'That is a pinnarist comment', said Hamish. 'Please withdraw it immediately'.

'And what if I don't, Mr Clever Mistoffeles. Will you report me to the Otic Guard? My dad works for them and they'd probably arrest you'.

Hamish realized there was no point in argument as they were outnumbered. They ran away, but not before Orwell had shouted 'bully cats are barely rats' in a rat-a-tat voice.

Samantha was very pleased to be rescued, but also surprised.

'Why did you come to help me, when I was so nasty to you only a short time ago?', she asked Orwell.

'We are just trying to be fair, and also trying to make sense of pinnarism. It is a very difficult subject. Very few cats seem to be able to talk about it without getting angry. But at least you were able to explain some of the reasons why small HO cats get so annoyed. It really was very helpful'.

Samantha smiled, a lovely smile that replaced her normal upturned nose. 'Why not come to our hut and have some milk and biscuits. Our family can all talk about this without getting upset.'

Hamish and Orwell were only too pleased to accept. They were in need of a restful end to their day. And to have tea with a micropinnate family would be a real bonus.

Chapter 10 The Otic Revolutionary Guard

There was another meeting planned for the next morning. The weather was drizzly and dull as Hamish and Orwell walked slowly to the headquarters of the Otic Revolutionary Guard. They were feeling drizzly and dull too; they had the feeling their questioning would not be well received at the centre of pinnarism control.

The Guard's headquarters were in an ugly concrete building at the edge of town. The Colonel of the Guard, Genghis Qualm, a well-built muscular Bengal with lots of medals on his chest, met them at the entrance.

'I have been waiting to see you. Word has passed around that you have been asking questions about pinnarism. You are on delicate territory here, I think, and I have already heard that you are getting close to trouble. Walls have HO's and my guards have been tuning in.

I want to put you straight right away. I am going to make it clear to you exactly how the Otic Revolutionary Guard functions and why it is necessary for the good of Felixtown. We have a set of clear principles; all of us should follow them. They are inscribed in the discs we always wear around our necks so we can never forget them. Do I make myself clear.'

Genghis produced two metal discs and pushed them towards Hamish and Orwell to read.

'As I am not sure how well you can read I am going to read them out to you now:

1. ***Pinnarism is wrong as it classifies cats by what they look like, not by how they are***
2. ***Pinnarism is offensive to all cats and those who practise it should be punished, if necessary by imprisonment***
3. ***Pinnarism is a source of temptation and needs to be stamped out by counter-measures***
4. ***Pinnarism can be identified through words, writing and behaviour***
5. ***The Otic Revolutionary Guard exists to identify and expose pinnarism***

Do you agree with all these? Most sensible cats do, pinnarist cats do not. Is there anything in these five principles that you object to. Don't be shy, say what you think'.

Hamish was worried. Genghis was making it very difficult for them to say what they thought. They could smell the possibility of arrest.

'Are you saying that if we disagree with any of these we are, by definition, pinnarist? It is very helpful having these five rules but can we ask questions about them separately?'

Colonel Qualm agreed. 'Go ahead. Our guards treat them all as one and, after you have asked your questions, I am sure you will both agree.'

Orwell piped up. He was determined to be careful for once.

'Nobody could possibly disagree with the first one. As my mum always taught me – a wise cat looks at another cat inside, not outside. It didn't make sense at first but it does now.'

'Good, that's a good start. What about the second?'.

Hamish was nervous about this one. It sounded too severe.

'I agree we cannot let pinnarism take over and we need some form of control. But this could come in lots of different forms. You could provide education, retraining, and rehabilitation instead of punishment.'

'They're just soft options', bristled Genghis. 'They don't work and, in any case, by the time these cats get to us, they are hard cases and have to be punished. 'Spare the whip and spoil the cat' is my motto. Most cats learn quickly when the red weals are throbbing in their bellies'.

Hamish and Orwell blanched. There was little point in arguing about this principle after this onslaught.

Genghis stormed ahead.

'And don't you agree that pinnarism is tempting to many cats with large HO's? It makes them feel superior, better than all the other cats, and a chance to be bossy and take over their lives.'

'That's a difficult one for us to answer', said Hamish. 'We both have large HO's and we have never felt superior to other cats, and that includes our brother, Torpedo, who had small HO's. But we are a little angry with some cats now as Torpedo has just been killed for no reason and we think pinnarism is behind it.'

'Well, there we are', Genghis said, very loudly. 'Your brother was killed by pinnarists who felt they had the right to take the law into their own hands and eliminate what they consider an inferior cat'.

'But if you respond by violence in dealing with pinnarism you perpetuate it. Is that really the way forward?'

'You, Hamish, are clearly a pacifist. But pacifists don't win wars, soldiers do'.

'Do you know what SS stands for?', asked Orwell out

of the blue.

Genghis became restless and uncomfortable.

'Why do you ask that?'

'It was just that we saw a badge near to where Torpedo was killed and it had 'SS' written on it'.

'I don't think you ought to worry about that. It could stand for all sorts of things. I prefer Sleepy Sundays; that's the day when I can put my front paws up and relax. But let's move on to the fourth rule. Do you agree that words, writing and behaviour can all aggravate pinnarism?

It was getting more difficult for Hamish and Orwell to agree with Genghis, but he was a very dominating figure.

Orwell could not contain himself here.

'The rule to abolish the use of the three-letter word that nobody can use now is stupid. I know I cannot say the word but if we continue on this path everybody is going to get confused. How can using the word be pinnarist? It's just a part of our anatomy, like paw, whisker and tail.'

Genghis was not pleased and although he tried to suppress it, he uttered a strangulated growl that sounded like twisting a cork in a bottle.

'I suggested that rule and will defend it to the last cat. We need to divert attention from the parts of our bodies that give rise to pinnarism and concentrate on our delightful faces, our brilliant sparkling eyes, our shiny coats, our elegant tails and beautifully adorned whiskers. In that way we take away all the poison that is attached to pinnarism and enjoy happy and fulfilling lives.'

Orwell thought he was listening to an advertisement for a cat beauty treatment; the only thing missing was the brand being sold, could it be 'Otic – the Scent of Seduction'. What Genghis was spouting was just cat walk fever. So he launched into dangerous territory.

'But we talk to communicate. If we hide words we don't inform, we just confuse. HO's are not the answer. I was listening to a friend the other day who was running a concert. He said he had enough tickets booked for eight shows. Nobody understood, as they all knew the concert was for cats but did not identify the number. Two valuable words were in danger of being lost to language. Is that a good thing?'

Genghis was now equally animated – and angry.

'You have failed completely to understand the awful power of wrong words. If you say that cats with small HO's are stupid, as I understand you have said on several occasions, this can be devastating – it can hurt and destroy lives as much as a claw to the throat.

Careless talk costs cat lives and this bring me on to the last of our principles. We at the Otic Revolutionary Guard exist to identify and expose pinnarism. We need to pick up the early stages of pinnarism before it spreads like a cancer and destroys society'.

'But if someone expresses a view, often in private, that is not publicly stated, and nobody complains is it right for you to take action against them?'

'Yes it is, and I will tell you a story to illustrate why. A kitten, we will call her Imelda, going to her first school last year said to another cat with small HO's, called Amelia, 'you should not be in my class'. Amelia was very upset by this but did not tell anybody about it at first. But she became more and more nervous about going to school and eventually was too frightened to attend. Her parents tried to make her go but she resisted and then stopped eating. In the end she starved herself to death and only mentioned Imelda's remark as she was dying'. We have remembered this. We call it Amelia's Retribution when training our new Guard members as it shows how a casual comment can lead to tragedy'.

'But how do you distinguish between an innocent comment implying 'you should not be in my class because you are too young' from the pinnarist one of 'you should not be in my class because you have short HO's?' Hamish was both curious and bothered.

'That's what our training is for. We do background checks on everybody and have a list of those who are potential pinnarists. So, once we suspect that a cat is a pinnarist we monitor them very closely over time – we call this due progress – and then wait for them to act or behave in a pinnarist way. Then we pounce and bring them here for questioning'.

Hamish and Orwell had now learned enough. They were not going to be persuaded by Genghis that his policies were right, and also gathered that if they asked the wrong questions they could easily be subjected to 'due progress'. So they thanked Genghis profusely for his time and made a rapid exit from the ugly building with its appropriately ugly notions.

As they left the building Orwell noted another hut in a hollow close by. He approached it. There was a sign with the same lettering on the badge he had found close to where Torpedo was killed. When they moved closer they saw the name Secret Service (SS) – No Admittance clearly marked on the gate.

'Look at that, Hamish. Sleepy Sundays indeed. I could tell Genghis was bothered when I mention SS. This is another branch of the Otic Revolutionary Guard, and it's obvious they want to keep it from the other cats in Felixtown.

At that moment a sentry came out of a side door.

'Move away. Visitors are prohibited here. Leave immediately or I will call the Guard'.

Hamish and Orwell galloped off. They were scared but angry. This place had something to do with Torpedo's death.

Chapter 11 Orwell is arrested

Orwell and Samantha were now close friends. Samantha liked his company and since the fight outside the hospital she had come to admire his courage and plain speaking. He also was great friends with Samantha's family and spent much time in their cosy hut in the centre of East Felixtown, a bustling neighbourhood where everybody seemed to be in a hurry.

But on this warm summer's day it was much quieter. Orwell was having a fish tea with Samantha in her hut. It was a little crowded with four kittens playing with wooden marbles on the floor, an older brother practising his jumps up a pole, and with Samantha's parents, Tabitha and Toby, keeping a constant eye on the tea, the table, the pole and the kittens to make sure nothing was knocked over. But Orwell felt very contented and pleased he had been accepted into this friendly household of cats with small HO's.

They were just about to finish when were three paw knocks on the door.

Tabitha came to the flap.

'It's a little late. What do you want?'

The face of an officer from the Otic Revolutionary

Guard filled the space where the flap had been.

'We are here to inform you that you are going to be moved to West Felixtown next week. The new accommodation is much larger than this tiny place and you will be very pleased with it'.

Tabitha, who always said what she thought without the filtering of reflection, was not especially pleased.

'We have no wish to move, thank you. We are happy here and all our friends live close by. Thank you for the offer, but no thank you, we do not want to leave'.

'Madam', said the officer, more severely now, 'this is not a suggestion, it is an order'.

Orwell was forced to intervene. He was always ready to jump in.

'Can I ask what is the reason for this request?'

'I can see you are not a member of this family as you are a macropinnate. Are you able to persuade the cats living here that it is in their interests to move to a bigger hut. This is a central part of the pinnarism project.'

'I am a friend of the family, but I am not here to influence them. They can make up their own minds'.

The officer curled back his lip to show an impressive, but unpleasant snarl and a set of shiny sharp teeth.

'I see. Another difficult family that needs to be persuaded. We will come back in the morning with my colleagues and all the papers to show you what you need to do. Please remember, this change is in your interest, especially to help you'.

The flap closed. The family all clustered round the table.

'I've heard about this'. Tabitha said. 'it's called the Relocation Project and some like it a lot as they are desperate to move. But we have made it clear we don't want to go. We're allowed to refuse, aren't we?'.

Orwell's tail bristled.

'I'm sure you can. But, just to make sure, I'll come back in the morning and support you. You will have noted they think I have more influence as I am a macropinnate, but they must be reminded that my influence, if greater, would be against the Pinnarism Constitution as we are all meant to be equal.'

The family was only too pleased for Orwell to return in the morning; they needed some help.

The next morning Orwell was at Samantha's hut early. The family were nervously waiting for the Otic Revolutionary Guard to visit again. Before long there was another tap on the flap to the entrance. Orwell looked out. There seemed to be a whole contingent of the Guard, Birmans with black faces and ears and menacingly blue eyes.

The same cat who visited the previous day seemed to be in charge.

'We are ready to escort you to your new residence. Have you packed all your belongings?'

Orwell had agreed to speak for the family.

'The family do not want to move. They made this clear to you last night. They are asking to be left alone'.

The snarl of the previous night appeared again.

'I wish make clear that you have no choice. All cats are going to be placed in places that ensures their equality. Do you not agree?'

"But the Feline Constitution states that 'equality and diversity can never be separated'. If that is true then those cats that have different opinions because of diversity can still be equal".

The Guard sneered.

'You are just making a play on words. That will get you nowhere'.

But Orwell persisted.

'Do you not remember the words of Skumbleshanks, the cat who owned Rudyard Kipling from humankind, and persuaded him to write "I am the cat that walks by himself and all places shall be alike to me". He was emphasising that cats have the choice to go their own way; they are independent. Does that not persuade you that choice is an essential requirement for all cats; they should not be dictated to by anyone'.

'We are not interested in humankind, especially colonial oppressors like Kipling who are pinnarists, so these words mean nothing to us. Now will you please get out of the way and let the family leave'.

Tabitha, Samantha and the rest of the family were cowed and frightened and moved towards the door to leave.

But Orwell stood in their way.

'You have not answered my question. A cat can choose to live in any place, at any time and in any way, and using force to prevent this is wrong'.

'That settles it', said the Guard. He blew a whistle and four Birman soldiers advanced to the hut.'

'I arrest this cat for obstructing us in our duty. Please take him to our headquarters before charging him and placing him in Felixtown Prison. The rest of you come with me. Your hut will be destroyed in twenty minutes.'

The four Birmans advanced and grabbed each of Orwell's legs in their teeth. He shouted as they dragged him to their Cat Rover. 'You cannot do this, you are preventing cat diversity, it is against the Constitution'.

'Do not listen to him, he is just a troublemaker' shouted their chief.' He is a pinnarist who is trying to get his own back, so if he continues to talk like this, gag him. He just spits poison against the cat revolution'.

Samantha, Tabitha and the four kittens came out of their hut sadly, carrying a blanket, two feeding bowls and a marble bag. They looked sadly at the Cat Rover as it left with Orwell struggling in the back. As it disappeared from view they trudged away under the guidance of the remaining Guard members to their new home in West Felixtown.

Chapter 12 Orwell on trial

Autumn was approaching. Orwell had been in prison for two months and the date of their trial had finally arrived. Old Dunstable was the judge in the case. He had asked to be recused as he knew Orwell but his reputation for integrity was so strong he was over-ruled. But he was not looking forward to the trial, especially as the two barristers involved, Sir Macup Fleece-Mog and Bella Belisha, were known for their strong opinions and robust questioning.

'Are you ready to begin your cross examination, Sir Macup?'. Old Dunstable nodded to the tall cat with a black gown.

Sir Macup Fleece-Mog arose from his chair, removed his wig, smoothed back his fur, already smooth, replaced his wig and put his paws on the lectern. The tension in the court was rising. He stared at Orwell.

'As you are very simple cat, Orwell, I will ask you one simple question. Do you, or do you not, agree with the first principle of the Feline Constitution, that 'all cats are created equal, with both having the unalienable rights of life, liberty and the pursuit of mice.'

'Yes'.

'Then why did you take it upon yourself to prevent a

deprived family from moving from East to West Felixtown, from a vermin infested hut to a newly built property. What possible excuse can you have for this behaviour.' He bared his teeth. 'Are you a spoilsport, a saboteur, or just a misguided adolescent?' He attempted a smile but his long thin face converted it to a sneer.

A faint cadence of gigglish mews from the Macup Fan Club fluttered round the court.

'None of these. I was standing up for cat rights, for diversity'.

'Diversity indeed. That's a long word for a very young cat. Do you know exactly what it means?'

'Yes, I do. It means allowing cats to be different'.

'I see'. Macup curled his lip. This was going to be fun. 'Interesting. So here you disagree with the Feline Constitution, in which equality is joined with diversity. You argue that you are showing diversity because you differ from the rest of us?'

'Yes'.

'So do you think it is your right, as a small and insignificant cat, to contradict the rest of the feline community?' He said 'feline community' as though it was a brick wall that could repel anything.

'I am standing up for cat freedom.'

Sir Macup rubbed his chin with a back paw. The rubbing noise went round the room. Fur was rising.

'So I understand you very well. You believe in freedom but not equality. Answer me this question. Would it not be better for an East Felixtown cat to grow up in a better neighbourhood with other cats in West Felixtown than to stay in squalor in the east?'

'Not if the cat wants to stay. I was standing up for the right to say no.'

'Ah, I see your logic now. You are saying that every cat has the right to contradict equality. So, if a kitten, probably with the same warped thinking that you are showing now, decided it did not want to be educated, it could opt out of going to school and stay at home chasing flies all day. Do you agree with that?'

'No, but you are twisting the truth'.

Macup was now angry. His fur bristled.

'How dare you say I am twisting the truth. I am a cat of distinction, you are just a disobedient miscreant, and you are in the dock'.

Orwell was equally annoyed.

'If I am right I would much prefer to be in the dock than in your chair.'

Old Dunstable intervened.

'It is not appropriate for you to abuse counsel. Please answer his questions politely.'

Macup was not pleased. He could tell he was not winning, so he changed tack.

'You are now getting impertinent. Do you not agree that, in obstructing the tasks of the Otic Revolutionary Guard, you were preventing the legitimate forces of Felixtown from carrying out their duty?'

'Yes, but that does not mean they were right'.

'Answer the question. Did you break the law?'

'Yes, I did'.

Macup smiled, his bristles settled and he smoothed his fur.

'Good. Members of the jury, please note his reply. He has admitted to breaking the law. I rest my case'.

There were a few seconds of silence before Old Dunstable invited the counsel to rise for the defence.

Miss Bella Belisha rose to her feet, her orange coat flashed brightly.

'I will not detain the court long. I intend to call two witnesses only. First, I call Tabitha Tymblehair'.

Tabitha came forward, somewhat nervously.

'Did you support Orwell when he tried to prevent your family from moving house?'

'Yes', answered Tabitha.

'Why did you not wish to move?"

'We are a simple family. We like living where we are, together with all our friends'.

'The town government has a policy of integrating housing so that nobody is disadvantaged. Do you agree with that?'

'Yes, in principle. But cats should have a choice and not to be forced to move'.

'Thank you. I now call on Samantha Tymblehair to testify'.

Samantha came up to the stand. She was more confident than her mother.

'Is your name Samantha and are you a member of Tabitha's family?'

'Yes'.

'Do you know Orwell?

'Yes, he is a friend of mine'.

'How long have you known Orwell for?'

'About six months. He was very helpful to me when I was attacked by other cats'.

'And did he offer to help you when your family was asked to move?'

'Yes. Orwell has very strong principles. He believes all cats should be allowed to be independent and should make their own decisions'.

Bella had finished.

'Thank you. Your witness, Sir Macup.' Bella smiled unctuously. Sir Macup strode up to the lectern in his manicured coat, smiling sardonically and raising his nose slightly to acknowledge the support of two of his nine sons, Septus and Nonus, as they leaned over the guard rail and mewed in support. Sir Macup was looking forward to grilling Samantha.

'Samantha. I am sure you are a very intelligent cat and at first I want to ask you a few questions that you will have no problem in answering. First, do you believe in rules?'

'It depends who makes them and what they are for'.

'And if a rule becomes law, should it be obeyed?'

'Yes'.

'And is it right for those who break rules that also happen to be laws that they should be punished?'

'Yes'.

'So you understand why your friend Orwell is in the dock. He has broken the law and should be punished'.

'But he has not really broken the law. He just tried to support us and stop us from being moved. If he has broken the law then we should all be punished as well'.

'I think you have been taken in, Samantha. I put it to you that you have been deceived by Orwell. He does not want your family to move to West Felixtown because he is a pinnarist. He pretends to be on your side but he does not want micropinnates in his part of town. It is as simple as that'.

'That is a lie and you know it'.

There was a shocked gasp in the court.

Old Dunstable had to intervene.

'Witness, you cannot accuse Sir Macup of lying. Please withdraw that comment'.

Samantha was now fully aroused. Her fur bristled all over her body and she became twice her size.

'I will not withdraw. I now know why he is called

Macup. He just makes up the evidence as he goes along. He has no interest in the truth'.

Old Dunstable persisted.

'If you do not withdraw that accusation you will be in contempt of court and will be arrested'.

'Go on then, arrest me. I am speaking the truth here even if all others are not'.

Old Dunstable had no choice.

'The witness will stand down and be taken away'.

Four Bengals grabbed Samantha by her front paws and dragged her away.

Old Dunstable coughed. He was not enjoying himself.

'I think we have now finished hearing the evidence - despite the interruption. Miss Belisha, would you like to make your closing statement for the defence.'

'Yes, your Honour. I will be fairly brief. Orwell has been accused of breaking the law by trying to prevent a family from being moved from East to West Felixtown. It is not in doubt that he obstructed the Otic Revolutionary Guard in their duties but in so doing he was only supporting a family with whom he had become close. The suggestion that he nefariously instilled himself into the family in order to prevent them from moving has absolutely no evidence in its favour and I will not refer to it again. Orwell, as has been observed already, is a cat who supports independent thinking. This does not mean that he ignores the wishes of society but that, he believes, wherever possible, cats should be allowed to go their own way. You will all know that condescending human expression about herding cats, making fun of us because we do not follow each other like sheep, and Orwell is clearly a cat in the non-herding tradition. If some activity seems too indistinguishable from blindly following sheep he asks questions, and, when Tabitha and her family were asked to move house against their will, he immediately stood up for them.

We know the Cat Constitution combines both equality and diversity but, in this case, they are not the same. Equality makes it clear that all cats should have similar living arrangements so that none are discriminated against, but diversity allows each cat to be different if he or she so chooses. I need to make one thing clear to the court. A cat may live in squalor if squalor living is chosen, provided there is no health risk. Tabitha and her family were far from living in squalor and their immediate environment was seen as beneficial. They should not have been moved without their agreement. I rest my case.'

Old Dunstable raised his left paw.

"Sir Macup, it is now time to hear your closing argument for the prosecution'.

Sir Macup, now not quite so calm, was ready. He turned towards the jury.

'Cats of the jury, the case before you is quite clear. An argumentative kitten, Orwell, has obstructed the lawful services of this town and has therefore committed an offence. You may have some sympathy with what he did but I would ask you to be very careful in how you interpret his evidence. He, and his consort, Samantha, have tried to convince you that he was acting in the best interests of the family in trying to prevent their move. But did you notice how vehemently they presented their case.'

He paused, for no reason apart for the wish to add dramatic effect to what followed.

'I am a student of cat psychology and have noted that when felines become ardent in making their views known there is usually something hidden behind their anger. They want to obscure their true feelings. I think that what Orwell has demonstrated is hidden or covert pinnarism'.

A gasp like a rippling wave went around the court.

'Yes, Orwell did not want Tabitha and her family to come to West Felixtown as he is a pinnarist at heart. But he knew he could not admit this and so made up this polecat and dog story about defending their right to be independent and stay where they were. You must remember we are still surrounded by pinnarists, cats who believe in the innate superiority of macropinnates. They can only show this indirectly and are getting very clever at hiding their true beliefs. We now have a large number of scholars who can identify pinnarism in the most bland of remarks – 'a cat may look at a king' is one of them, as you must have noticed all the royal images are of cats with large HO's. So, we need to root out pinnarism from every corner of Felixtown. I am now sure you will not only agree that Orwell is guilty but that he deserves a long sentence. This will send a message to all the other pinnarists who are competing for our support in their underhand, secretive and evil ways'.

Sir Macup delvered the last sentence dramatically with both front paws raised and pointing forward with their claws extended. He wanted visual as well as verbal reinforcement.

Old Dunstable sighed. He was glad the trial was over.

'The court is now adjourned. We will meet again when the jury is ready to deliver their verdict.'

....
....

Two hours later the jury returned. Once all had resumed their seats Old Dunstable stood up.

'Have you reached a verdict?', he asked the foreman, a Burmese cat of sparse elegance.

'Yes'.

'Is this a verdict on which you all agree?'

'Yes'.

'Do you find the prisoner, Orwell, guilty or not guilty of the charge of obstructing the Otic Guard?'

'Guilty'.

'Thank you', said Old Dunstable. You may now lie down'.

He called Orwell back into the dock.

'Orwell, you have been found guilty of obstructing the Otic Revolutionary Guard in the execution of their duties. As this is your first offence I am sending you to a re-education centre instead of prison. The sentence is for six months and there will be no early release. I hope you will benefit from your rehabilitation and will not offend again'.

Sir Macup scowled. His recommendation was being ignored.

Orwell, expecting a prison sentence, was relieved. As he was escorted out of the court he made his front paws into the shape of a heart and smiled at Samantha. She waved back. He was proud of himself for not buckling. Cats like him were not bucklers but fighters for cat rights.

Chapter 13 Hamish is attacked

Hamish was distressed following Orwell's imprisonment. Torpedo had been killed, probably murdered, and in their task of investigating pinnarism he and Orwell had seemed to encounter nothing but trouble. Pinnarism as a solution to the problems of cat society was not the answer. It had created many more problems than it had ever solved. Why had such a sensible project gone off the rails?

Mum could understand it even less so than Hamish. 'You have always been such a sensible and happy kitten. I blame myself for asking you to investigate pinnarism. It's led to Orwell going to prison. If I had kept my mouth shut it would never have happened.'

Hamish was now getting to the view that pinnarism was becoming a menace to cat society, an irrelevant and unnecessary stain infecting all with a mixture of anger and fear. The principle behind it was sound but the way it was being implemented was causing nothing but havoc, and everybody seemed to be under suspicion. Even the most innocent of comments could be judged as pinnarist in the way it was said, to whom it was addressed, and how many were listening. So, when a teacher said to a class of lazy kittens, 'your homework is pathetic, you are learning nothing, and if you continue in this way you will all fail in hunting', he was reported to the Revolutionary Guard by a parent. Most of the class were micropinnates; the teacher was accused of pinnarism and lost his job. How could this be just?

He was now spending many more evenings outside home trying to make sense of what he had learnt, how it could be used positively, and agonising how cats might discuss the subject without crossing into conflict. The whole subject of pinnarism was now toxic; Wilberforce Shorthair could never have expected this when he launched his campaign with such optimism only sixteen months ago.

On one warm June night he was by the copse close to home and resting in an old badger sett. He was in the curious state that all cats had before they go to sleep, dozing but still sensitive to any unusual stimulus. But he must have drifted off into sleep. He surfaced to feel a large snarling body on top of him... He thought at first it must be a badger coming back to the sett but then he quickly realised it was another cat, the smell was unmistakable.

Hamish struggled and lashed out with his teeth and claws. He was being smothered. Whoever was attacking him was equally persistent and would not let go. The two cats were now locked together, rolling over and over in a tight ball like sparring hedgehogs, scattering their fur among the crackling beech leaves on the ground. Hamish soon realised this was a fight to the death; the other cat was not going to give up or run away. As they rolled over and over Hamish gradually moved his mouth closer to the other cat's neck, but at the same time he realised the other cat was trying to do the same. He could feel his windpipe being compressed; he could not breathe and was getting weak. Then, in a desperate lunge he a bit as hard as he could on the other cat's throat. Within a few seconds the other cat, who had been holding his body in a vice, had released his grip and flopped to the ground.

Hamish slowly turned over to look at whoever had made this unprovoked assault. It was clear that whoever it was had stopped breathing and was now dead. Hamish took a closer look. Wow. This cat was none other than Groubadour Fernandez, the black shorthair that had long been a bully in their community.

Hamish looked more closely. He noticed a small badge attached to his collar. 'SS' it read, just like the one that he had found close to where his brother Torpedo had been killed.

But he could not take it all in. He was weak and now noticed a large bloody gash in his upper thigh. He had to get back home and stop the bleeding, but now he was now exhausted and very weak. He struggled back along the path to home, with every step making him wince in agony. Finally, he was able to limp back and come into the kitchen at home.

Mum was there.

In situations like this she said little but knew exactly what to do.

'Stay still, Hamish, don't say anything. I'm going to look after you'. She grabbed him by the scruff of his neck and made him lie flat. She stretched and exposed the wound on his thigh by cleaning and licking it repeatedly until all the dirt and fur had been removed. She then persuaded him to lie on a soft bed of muslin and gave him some milk. All this was done in complete silence. When first aid was most important there was no time to talk.

But after a short time Hamish had recovered enough and Mum was able to find out what had happened.

'Who did this, Hamish? What on earth were you doing?'

'It was Groubadour Fernandez, Mum, he attacked me when I was half asleep. I have no idea why. I always knew that cat was a menace and I'm quite convinced now that either he, or one of his friends, must have murdered Torpedo.'

'And where is he now?'

'He's over in the wood but now I think he's dead'.

Mum was now highly alarmed.

'Stay there. I'm going to check. If he's alive we need to save him'.

She ran out of the house and followed Hamish's scent to the badger sett. But there was nothing there apart from a few blood stains. She returned quickly.

'Why do you think he's dead, Hamish? I found the place where you were fighting but he wasn't there.'

Hamish was convinced Groubadour was dead but was too tired to argue. His mind was becoming unscrambled; the attack was not just an isolated one. The SS badges near to where Torpedo was killed, and the one Groubadour was wearing, were not a coincidence. The strange experience they had when they saw the Secret Service headquarters next to the Otic Revolutionary Guard headquarters had showed them there was another part to the Guard that very few knew about. The Secret Service was indeed a secret service and, whatever it was concerned with, it was also involved in murder. But making sense of it all was now too difficult. He just had to get some sleep.

Chapter 14 . The Re-education of Orwell

Orwell was brought into the re-education room. It was bare apart from a large sign on the wall:

"Be careful what you share: pinnarists are everywhere"

A smiling tortoiseshell sat in front of the sign. Orwell thought she looked overweight, soapy and constipated, but he was in a bad mood so nothing about her appearance could have pleased him.

'Good morning, Orwell. My name is Maisie. I hope you are looking forward to this enterprise'.

Orwell was not to be taken in.

'I cannot look forward to something that has been given to me as punishment'.

'Come, come now. This is not a punishment. This is to help you to come to an understanding of pinnarism and lead you to be more comfortable in supporting our constitution. Our programme has three parts, the identification of pinnarist ideas you may have unwittingly learnt, their removal, and their replacement with forward looking anti-pinnarism beliefs.

I will start by asking you a few standard questions.

What is your view about the life and works of Rum Tum Lugger?'

'It is mixed. I do not like the way he exploited micropinnates and many other cats, or his building of slave ships to bring them over here. But I thought his adoption of the cat chronometer that allowed the ships to navigate better, was a good thing and I admire him for that.'

'Thank you. And now my second question; do you think pinnarism in the past should be judged in the same way as pinnarism today?'

'No, not at all. Cats in the past had different morals and habits from those of today. So, if pinnarism was part of normal society and everyone followed its rules it must have been different from today'.

Maisie's tail bristled, but she continued.

'Do you think there should be reparations, or similar forms of apology, from cats with large HO's to those with short HO's because of the way they have been treated in the past?'

'No, absolutely not. What's done is done. When cats almost wiped out the population of rabbits two centuries ago, we all cheered then. We now think that was uncivilised behaviour but do not think it necessary to apologise to rabbits for being such good predators in the past'.

'We have completed the first section of my questions – the history of pinnarism. I am sorry to say that you failed on all three questions. You must have been taught about Rum Tum Lugger's work on the cat chronometer at school but this has now been removed from the syllabus. Pinnarism is morally wrong and differences in attitudes and behaviour in the past do not excuse it, morals are not flexible, they are fixed. Historical pinnarism is no different from current pinnarism.

So let us see if you do better with my questions on education'.

She gave an acid smile with the corners of her mouth turned down; it made Orwell shudder.

'Why do micropinnates have fewer successes in exams than macropinnates?'

'It's because their hopes and wishes in life are not focused on academic subjects. Their culture gives more credit to sporting success and other physical activities.'

Maisie curled her whiskers and continued.

'Are micropinnates then less intelligent than macropinnates?'

'It depends how you measure intelligence. If you take all measures they are similar'.

'My last question. Why are there so few micropinnate professors at Felixtown University?'

'It's down to ambition. Macropinnates think it is the height of success to be a professor, micropinnates regard the Marble Championship as much more important. They have a different scale of eminence. I am sure mine is different from yours'.

Maisie shook her head.

'We are not here to test my views. Yours are at issue, and it is clear you are definitely in need of help, Orwell. The correct answer to all my questions is a simple one, pinnarism, but this seems to have slipped your mind. Or perhaps, and much more dangerous, it has taken over your thinking.

My last set of questions will test your beliefs.

Do you think you are a superior cat?'

Orwell thought carefully.

'I do not compare myself as a whole with other cats. I am superior in some matters, inferior in others'.

Maisie nodded.

'And do you think you have greater knowledge than micropinnates?'

'I have more knowledge in some subjects, less in

others. The question does not mean anything'.

'And what do you believe is the major problem affecting cat society today?'

Orwell knew perfectly well what Maisie wanted him to say, but he was not going to play along with it. He had been honest until now; he was not going to change.

'It is a lack of tolerance. We are told we have to praise cat diversity but we are doing the opposite. We are forcing everybody to think and talk in the same way. It will not work. Cats are going to think in their own ways, to walk and talk in their own ways, and go through life in their own ways. That is their nature and you will not be able to change it no matter how hard you try'.

Maisie shook her head slowly and stared at him.

'You are a very stubborn cat, Orwell. But we have come across cats like you before. We are going to place you in cell 102 of this reformatory. This is where you will learn and inwardly digest the philosophy of anti-pinnarism that is currently so lacking in your nature. In 102 you will come face to face with your ignorance and your stupidity. But we do not despair. After your retraining you will be a fine cat in our society. But you are far away from that at present, Orwell. You are out on a limb and I can now understand why you have been HO-marked for re-education. You need it more than any other cat I have ever known.'

Maisie gave a high-pitched mew and two Manx orderlies appeared.

'Cell 102, please', said Maisie. 'Make sure he has the full regime'.

The two orderlies beckoned to Orwell and he followed them down a long corridor, at the end of which was a flap covering a tiny opening. Orwell was shown in. He was in a space measuring about 3 feet square. It was completely bare, with floor, walls and ceiling in a chilling uniform grey.

He attempted to be cheerful.

'Nice place for a doze, but what else am I expected to do?'

'Nowt', grunted one of the orderlies. 'Lessons start later'.

They left after closing the flap.

Orwell sighed. This was not going to be an easy time for him but he was determined to be strong. He kept thinking of Torpedo. He would want his brother to be proud of him.

....

Orwell was exhausted. He was short of sleep – the Room 102 system only allowed 6 hours sleep before the tannoy woke him and the other prisoners with its yowling at 5 in the morning – and he was bereft mentally, the repeated barrage of recordings followed by him having to repeat the vacuous mantra 'pinnarism is bad, pinnarism is evil and pinnarism must never be tolerated' after every session of re-education. This useless chant was called the Consolidation, the belief that if you said the same comment, whether sensible or stupid, over and over again it became the truth.

He had been through the ten sessions of Critical Pinna Theory, the review of cat history that had been recorded by pinnarists ever since the Domesday Tract. This teaching had drummed in into him, over and over, that the pinnarist chroniclers had been biased and had deliberately left out all the great contributions to society made by micropinnates, most of which were in mew recordings that only some micropinnates could understand. The history textbooks were being rewritten to correct all the errors but it would take many years to record the truth.

After Critical Pinna Theory Orwell had been immersed in Cat Quality and Diversity Training, beginning with a set of lectures by Maisie on Hidden Prejudice, Pinnarist Language, Power Assumptions, Executive Privilege and Casual Authority. Each of these was given its prominence in capital letters but Orwell quickly realised they were all the same.

Hidden prejudice was not really hidden; if you said to a micropinnate, 'I know you won't understand this', even if was about a specialist subject like cat calorie mathematics, you were accused of pinnarism by implication. Pinnarist language was almost identical, as it allowed any statement that implied, or even vaguely hinted at, superiority of a macropinnate over a micropinnate to be labelled as pinnarist. By extension, any suggestion of macropinnate superiority in a feline interaction was stamped as a Power Assumption. Similarly, any cat with large HO's who was in a position of authority over a cat with small HO's had to be excessively careful not to say anything that could be seen as Executive Privilege or pinnarist Casual Authority. So, the exercise was like a continuous game of Snakes and Ladders; every time you climbed up a ladder you found it impossible to avoid a pinnarist statement that sent you down the board again.

The last part of the training was a set of multiple-choice questions called Detecting Pinnarism in Other Cats. Orwell quickly relabelled this The Snitch's Charter. An extremely observant cat, fully trained in all aspects of pinnarism, was able to identify from simple statements all the features of fully fledged pinnarism. Orwell found all the questions amusing in their ludicrous construction and he found one quite fascinating:

A teacher is instructing a cat with small HO's in the art of cooking. Which of the following statements is pinnarist?

1. *'You must forget about all you have learnt before and just follow what I do'.*
2. *'Do not eviscerate the rat before cooking'.*
3. *'I apologise if you have not come across scallops before'.*
4. *'This recipe comes from the Cat Breed Cookbook published 100 years ago.'*

Orwell thought none of the answers indicated any hint of pinnarism but knew he had learnt to dig deep when exploring the secret tunnels of pinnarism. So he was able to produce the response that all four statements indicated pinnarism. If you asked a cat with small HO's to forget part of their past culture, whether in cooking or anything else, you were pinnarist; if you uses macropinnate words like 'eviscerate' you were being patronising to micropinnates who might not understand them; if you apologised about something that you thought might be outside the experience of a micropinnate you were immediately exposing your pinnarism. Once you needed to apologise your secret views were exposed – a cat with short HO's was assumed to be ignorant of fish delicacies such as scallops whether or not it was true. Finally, if you quoted from a very old book, it was almost certainly written by a macropinnate and so could be discounted as genuine knowledge. So pinnnarism was in the air, in the culture and in everybody's spoken words.

After he reflected a little Orwell had a sudden realisation. Anti-pinnarism, or posotism as it was now called, was not a project, not a policy, not a programme, it was a religious cult. At its core was the fundamental belief that all the problems in feline society stemmed from pinnarism and once this was removed all cats would be in the promised land. Although this was dressed up as science or as evidence it was not; it was a belief and only those who embraced it completely had true faith. This allowed its disciples to see pinnarism everywhere, in simple interactions between cats, in written or spoken communication, and in ordinary feline behaviour. A whisker raised, a back arched, a paw waved, a tail rotated, all could be interpreted as evidence of covert pinnarism. It was also singularly lacking in humour. Jokes were usually viewed as pinnarism in disguise, and if you laughed at them, you were a pinnarist suspect. What Orwell and others in Cell 102 were going through under the guise of re-education was better described as indoctrination. It was a plan to grind out all the vestiges of pinnarist attitudes, thinking and language. Any cat that still had doubts about the purpose of this indoctrination would continue to be grilled, bullied and manoeuvred into this alternative path until true understanding was achieved.

Before Orwell could absorb this insight fully he was interrupted by the door flap opening. A rough looking cat of uncertain breed with lively eyes was pushed inside.

'You can join another of your tribe in there until you learn sense'. Orwell recognized the muffled voice of the Manx orderly. The flap closed and the visitor greeted Orwell with a brief nose rub.

'Hello, I'm Mansoor, but I'm called Mansi for short.'

'Nice to see some friendly whiskers again. But why have they put you with me?'

'Simple. They've run out of room as so many cats need to be re-educated. They're just pouring in now. Pinnarism is being detected in every corner. I'm glad I'm not an otologist at one of those clinics; I don't know how they avoid being rounded up. They have to talk in code all day'.

'And how did you offend?'

'I just lost it one day. I work for the Feline Hunting Society and most of my pupils are very good, for as you know we cats are all highly motivated here. But I had one cat, who by chance had small HO's, who kept on insisting that cats could climb down trees as easily as climbing up them. He produced all sorts of phony explanation such as 'it must be true because otherwise many cats would die at the tops of trees'. That doesn't alter the fact that climbing up is much easier than climbing down and in the end I got so exasperated, I said,'if you really believe that you're a Roundhead.'

'A Roundhead? I haven't come across that before'.

'No, not many have. Many years ago in the Cat Battle Era the Roundheads ran the show. They were very stolid cats who were well-disciplined but who had limited imagination and could be well trained into a model army. They had large round faces and very small HO's so they quickly picked up the nickname of Roundheads. Of course, this comment, even though it was half a joke and half a telling off, was immediately passed on to the Otic Guard and I was arrested the next day. I hadn't got much of a defence – when I said it was a joke they became very angry – and so here I am'.

Mansi continued to explain why the Otic Guards were running out of space to accomodate all the pinnarism offenders.

'In the past you used to get a fine or a community order for pinnarist offenders. Now they come down on you – we are all malicious offenders and need educating again in equality and diversity, those ridiculous words that have about as much meaning as bread and jam. They've got it into their heads that pinnarism is like a parasitic worm; once it gets into your body as inappropriate language it can take over your mind. But if it continues along this path they will run out of space at prisons, re-education centres and all types of corrective institutions and the country will just judder to a halt'.

Mansi continued to sound off against the stupidity of the Otic Revolutionary Guard. He described how members of the Guard had been place in schools to detect what were called 'early alien traces', ways of thinking, talking or writing that indicated the cats concerned had been infected with pinnarist notions. These had to be stamped out at an early stage if they were not to take over all parts of behaviour. His own son had almost been incriminated as he had said in a biology lesson that corn could be distinguished from many other plants by its ears. Even though the ears of corn have no connection with the HO's of cats this was immediately detected by the guard at the back of the class and he was called in for language correction. He got out of it by telling the guard that some of the time he was saying the word 'hairs' rather than ears, so after an admonishment he was allowed to go.

Orwell and Mansi continued their conversation into the night. Nothing was held back. They did not have to add caution to their comments; they were completely in tune with each other and in talking with complete freedom about all the ridiculous, stupid, crazy aspects of pinnarism across Felixtown it was as though a heavy weight had been lifted off their backs and they could think of hope again. Their companionship would help them weather the storms ahead.

Chapter 15 The Secret Service arrests Hamish

There was bound to be comeback following the death of Groubadour. Although Mum continued to argue that he must have survived as he was no longer in the wood, Hamish was convinced that the only way Groubadour could have disappeared was by his body being removed. But who would have done this? It must have been The Secret Service. This was a network organised by the state and clearly had many members who worked together. Others must have known that Groubadour was going to try and kill Hamish and so were on hand to check what had happened after the assault.

So, he could only wait and be ready for any response.

It came four days later. An early morning knock on the door was followed by a contingent of the Otic Revolutionary Guard piling up at the door so they blotted out the light.

'We have come to interview Hamish. He needs to accompany us now', barked the Birman in charge.

Mum was worried but also very annoyed.

'What are you trying to do? My middle son, Torpedo, has been murdered, my youngest one, Orwell, has been arrested and convicted, quite unfairly in my lights, and now you come to take my remaining son away. You might as well arrest me as well. You'll have completed the job then'.

'Don't argue with them, Mum. They are under instructions from others. I'll find out from whom when I have had my interview.'

Hamish packed his tiny belongings -cats always need very little – and left with the Guard. He recognised some of the places they passed – the hospital, the library, the police station – but he was not taken to any of them. As he was being taken by the Otic Revolutionary guard he presumed he would finish up at their headquarters. But he did not. He was taken to a dilapidated hut at the corner of the town. It was unsigned and looked as though it has been a fish warehouse in the past.

Indeed, when Hamish was inside he was convinced he could smell haddock.

He was taken to a room where two grey cats were sitting behind a large map of Felixtown on the floor.

'We have been asked to interview you by the Special Service of the Otic Revolutionary Guard. They have reason to believe that you have been involved in pinnarist activities that may have led to the death of one of their staff. '

Hamish decided it was best to act dumb.

'I have no idea what you were talking about but I'm happy to answer any questions you may ask. I have nothing to hide.'

'One of our detectives, Groubador Fernandez, who works in the Special Service, was found dead a short distance away from your home on the 20th of June. We have reason to believe that you were involved in his death'.

'I do not have the slightest idea what you were talking about. I am only too willing to help you but have nothing to go on'.

'We will start by asking a few questions and would ask you to be very careful in your replies. Did you know Groubador Fernandez?'

'Yes, I came across him twice'.

'Were you friends with him?'

'No. He was a bully'.

'Did you meet him on the night of the 20th of June?'

'No, I did not meet him'.

'Where were you on the night of the 20th of June?'

'I was at home with my mother'.

'Did you have any contact with Groubador Fernandez?'

'No, I do not know what you are insinuating'.

'We have reason to believe that you were responsible for, or at least were involved with, the death of Groubador. As you are clearly not helping our enquiries you will be placed under house arrest and we will question you later.'

He turned to his colleagues.

'Take him away to Hut 8. We have the technology there to test if he is lying.'

Three guards placed pelvic manacles on Hamish's paws and he was hauled away.

Chapter 16 Hut 8

Hamish paced up and down in Hut 8. The room was only the size of 50 square cat baskets and after five days he was familiar with every inch. There was a board with flashing lights at the end of the room which meant nothing to him. He had been told it was there to 'find the truth', but apart from making him feel intimidated it seems to have no purpose. He looked out of the only window to see the micropinnate sentry sitting on the wall, half asleep for most of the time as he had so little to do. He had now been in Hut 8 for five days. It was wearing him down.

He could not decide whether to tell the truth. Perhaps the flashing lights were having an effect on his thinking. He was murderously attacked by Groubador and he was very lucky to be alive. So why not admit that he killed Groubador in self-defence instead of denying he had any contact with him.

In the end he decided this was probably the best way to respond. If the Special Service were responsible for sending Groubador to kill him they would obviously deny this. But then they would have to provide some explanation of why and how Groubador came to see him, and this would not be easy to avoid them being implicated. After pacing round and round the hut he had determined the way forward; he would say exactly what happened, appeal for mercy and hope for the best. As he settled down after making this decision he noticed the flashing lights on the board had disappeared.

Chapter 17. The Amnesty

Five days had passed, long tedious days. Hamish had not yet been interviewed or charged. He was expecting to be charged with murder. So, he had rehearsed his defence carefully. He suffered an unprovoked attack, had defended himself and, if he had not bitten Groubadour, he himself would have perished.

But why had he not been charged? He could only wait for the inevitable. Like all cats finding themselves in situations where they were helpless, he turned to the standard solution enshrined in the Cat Constution, curled-up sleepfulness. He stretched out completely and within a few seconds was fast asleep.

He awoke to hear a rustling outside the hut. He looked out of the window and in the distance he could see sentries moving up and down between the huts. Some of the doors were being opened and the cats inside were coming out. Many more official cats in red markings appeared and before long they had opened all the huts.

'Please come to Hut 8 too', mouthed Hamish to himself. 'Don't forget me. I don't want to be last in, last out'.

He did not have long to wait. A large Maine Coon cat

with impressive ears dressed in red epaulettes was approaching Hut 8. He carried great authority and, despite his large HO's, it was clear pinnarism had not ground him down. The door opened.

Hamish was dazzled by the sun as he had been cooped up for so long, and blinked as tears ran down his face.

'Are you Hamish and have you been detained here by the Secret Service?', asked the Maine Coon in a firm voice.

'Yes, I am. Can I ask what is happening here?'

'I am authorised by Wilberforce Shorthair to grant an amnesty to you and, what is more, for you to receive an apology from him in due course. The Secret Service has been found to be operating against the law in breach of the Cat Constitution and will be closed down immediately. You have been detained unlawfully'.

Hamish ran out of the hut and jumped so high he almost landed on the dozing sentry on the wall, who was still half asleep in the sun. He grabbed his belongings and skipped out of the hut. There was much to do and first he must find out if Orwell had been released too.

He did not have long to wait. As he threaded his way through Felixtown to the re-education unit there were many more cats on the street and they seemed much happier than he had ever seen them before. Quite a few were just skittering around in circles in a sort of mesmerising dance. But a few figures stood around looking puzzled and unhappy; some seemed to have the trimmings of the Otic Revolutionary Guard.

'What's going on here?', he asked a particularly excited Persian with a conical purple hat on his head.

'The pinnarism nonsense is over. I had chronic earache but now its gone away. Hooray for all ears, wherever they are and whatever their sizes. This is Ear Liberation Day'.

And then Hamish spied Orwell and Samantha in the distance among another group of revellers, dancing in the individual sinuous and seductive way that cats have made their own. Great, they must have been released too.

He-ran over towards them and after ten minutes of sinuous nose rubbing they were able to recap at least some of what had happened.

Orwell had found out from Mansi that Wilberforce Shorthair was getting unhappy as he had received nothing but a mass of negative news about the Pinnarism Project. It had become so toxic that he had convened a special meeting of his Cabinet. It was not clear what had happened there but it led to the immediate abandonment of the project, followed by the decision to disband the Otic Revolutionary Guard.

The vague message had filtered through that it was not the principle of the project that had been abandoned but the way it was being executed. Mansi said these were weasel words to avoid the loss of face, but it was very clear there had been many concerns that the project was increasing conflict in cat society. The decision was made that the project could no longer be tolerated in the form that it was set up; nobody could say it was working well.

All this was the most delightful music to Hamish's ears. Somehow the message got through that the Pinnarism Project was a mistake; it has made society more suspicious, angry and combative, turning cat against cat. He and Orwell knew that already; it was so pleasing to hear of this now being appreciated across catworld.

They all had to celebrate. There must be a party, and, sure enough, the staff at the East Felixtown Assembly Hall had already anticipated this. They had even brought in the inventors of the Cheshire Cat Dance to set up a special show, and nobody wanted to be let out of that. The Dance had come about after reading a human story from the mists of time. It starts with all the cats making a large oval ring. Then, at the sound of a whistle, the hairless cats, the Sphinxes, Bambinos and Devon Rexes, crowd into the ring and lie down, adjusting themselves so that together they make the rounded shape of a cat's body. After a few more circuits the tabbies and tortoiseshells move into the ring and lie among the hairless cats, adding fur to the Cheshire Cat, and the American Shorthairs, the Maine Coons and the Chartreux join at the back to make a long tail. After more dances around the cat the Forest and Rag Doll cats with their long whiskers create the mouth and face of the Cheshire Cat and fashion it into a long and satisfying smile.

All this was carefully created in the Assembly Hall, as it had been many times before the Pinnarism Project had been set up. Once the Cheshire Cat was complete, the start whistle blew and the cats in the ring danced round it to the clanking music of the cat xylophones, faster and faster, until the whistle blew again. Then the tail cats peeled off, followed by the tabbies and tortoiseshells and the hairless cats making the body. Finally, the cats at the head also left, but all making sure that at the end only a large whiskered smile remained.

The Dance finished with all the cats apart from those making the smile in the ring, chanting in unison:

'Cheshire, Cheshire, show us the style

Cheshire, Cheshire, all us beguile

Cheshire, Cheshire, let us join the queue

Cheshire, Cheshire, make us smile like you'

Only the Cheshire Cat Dance could expunge the worries and troubles of the last two years. They repeated it, and again, and continued dancing until the early morning hours, before Orwell and Samantha, nestling in each other's paws, collapsed with Hamish and a myriad of other cats down on the floor, where they entered the deepest and most satisfying of feline sleeps that would be the envy of all other animals.

Chapter 18 The Pinnarism Commission Writes A Letter

Hamish and Orwell felt they had to go and talk to somebody at the top about the sudden change in pinnarist policy. It was all very welcome news but there was no explanation. Mum told them not to worry; 'it's all come out well, possibly because of your help. I'm very proud of you both. I'm sure Torpedo would have been too. So, there is no need to do anything more. We can just get ahead with our lives now. I've got heartily fed up with all the new-isms, I want to go back to an old one, optimism. That's good enough for me.'

There had been talk about the setting up of a special commission to examine the Pinnarism Project but very few seemed to be aware of who was involved and what were its terms of reference. But perhaps this commission might have been involved in the change in policy.

A few days later a letter arrived that helped everybody to appreciate that the Pinnarist Commission had not been idle.

THE PINNARISM AGREEMENT

This letter in being sent to all cats in the four counties as it explains the changes that will take place immediately in the Pinnarism Project. This follows an extensive examination of the work of the Project, carried out by the ten members of the Commission, half of whom are micropinnates and the other half of macropinnates. The Commission has recommended the following changes, to be implemented immediately:

1. The word 'ear' and all other words related to hearing are no longer excluded from feline communication and can be used whenever appropriate.
2. All allegations of pinnarism should be made in writing to the Pinnarism Commission. Those approved as pinnarist will be published every month with the names of the accuser and accused included.
3. Pinnarism is now a legal term and pinnarist allegations will only be supported if, after legal advice, they are considered to demonstrate malice, discrimination or intent to harm.
4. Innocent inappropriate use of language is no longer regarded as pinnarist.
5. Allegations of historical and colonial pinnarism in the context of scholarship and learning are

not to be regarded as pinnarist. Revision of old texts to exclude writings viewed as pinnarist will stop immediately.

Although these changes will take place immediately they are not final. A national vote will be held on 22nd May, C1013 and, if there is a 'Yes' vote in favour of these recommendations they will be incorporated into feline law.

Thank you for reading this letter, and please vote on 22nd May.

Wilberforce Shorthair, Prime Minister

Chapter 19 Sagacity explains

Hamish and Orwell were very pleased with the letter and were determined to get all their friends to vote for the Agreement, just over a month away. But they were still puzzled at the magnitude of the change. The opportunity to know more came from a surprising invitation from Sagacity to have tea with him. The invitation included the words 'to thank for your help in clarifying recent events'. This was very pleasing, but also very mysterious. What had they done to help. They had just gone around Felixtown being nosy and had provided a report on their travels that nobody seemed to have read, as they had never received any acknowledgement.

Mum was overjoyed.

'They haven't forgotten you at all. You must have made a big impression on all of them. Now go and enjoy yourself at the tea and don't get into any arguments about any of the 'isms.' '

So, five days later Hamish and Orwell climbed up the hill to the *Let Wisdom Guide* entrance to Sagacity's house. Sagacity came out to greet them with an elaborate set of nose rubs which left a few marmalade hairs on Hamish's face. They made him look very wise but Orwell only giggled again – he always did when

Hamish looked pompous.

'Come straight in, we have a fine tea for you, salmon and roe fritters. I'm sure you'll like them'. He made sure they were comfortably seated before joining them with the food, served on elegant shell trays.

'You may be surprised to receive this invitation. But you shouldn't be, as your report was of great value to the Pinnarism Commission. Almost all the information the Commission received from others could be described as obvious and unconstructive. In short, it was soporific, and, as you know, it does not take much to send a cat off to sleep. These other reports were very careful in their language as they were frightened to offend. You just described everything as you found it, and this made it clear to us that many senior cats in Felixtown were very dissatisfied in the way the pinnarism project was developing. They paid cat lip service to it, which although soothing and fitting in with official policy, still showed an undercurrent of unhappiness that your report brought out very well.'

'But we can't have had much impact on the recommendations, as they were so broad. They completely upended all the standard pinnarism rules', said Hamish.

'No, of course not', said Sagacity, 'but your report showed that all were ready for change'.

Orwell continued to be puzzled.

'There must have been a lot more going on. You must have more you can tell.'

Sagacity took a deep breath and invited them to nibble another fritter.

'There were four reasons why the Pinnarism Project as envisaged by Wilberforce Shorthair had to be abandoned; its effect on the economy, the growth of posotism, the loss of learning and the growth of violence. None of these had been predicted in that idealistic dawn of two years ago.'

'The economy?', said Oscar. "How could that be so important? What has pinnarism got to do with money? I did not think ears had cash value'.

'Yes, they have. Quite simply, more and more work and energy was going into stamping out pinnarism, and this was not productive. There should have been economic gain as micropinnates became more involved in cat society but it simply did not happen. I will try and explain why.'

Sagacity cleared his throat and shook himself. A few marmalade hairs rose and slowly floated to the ground'

'When Wilberforce introduced his initiative the gross product of Felixtown was 11 million pawnees as most of the workforce was active in production or helping other cats. With the growth of pinnarism more than a fifth of the workforce was diverted into the prevention of, or punishment for, pinnarism and this earned no pawnees at all. So, everybody's standard of living has fallen, there is less food available, cats have stopped reproducing as looking after kittens was too expensive, and so everything was going into a steep decline. It we had continued on the same path we would become a 'cuanagaro republic', named after the ocelots in Venezuela who are always in debt and a state of total chaos. So, we had to spend more wisely. That meant getting rid of the financial burden of pinnarism'.

'Was posotism a drain on finances too?', asked Hamish.

'Absolutely', replied Sagacity. 'As I mentioned to you when I first met you, posotism was noted to be a relatively minor problem then but has since taken over vast areas of feline life. Revenge has a long pedigree. So many cats with small ears with resentment burning in their families for generations were determined to get their own back. But the consequence was that more and more cats who had large ears were deprived of the jobs in which they were highly productive and replaced by cats with small ears. Some of these new arrivals were good, but many others were appointed mainly because they had small ears and this took precedence over everything else. So if a rather dim small eared cat was unfairly promoted over a highly productive one with large ears the country again suffered. Even those with small ears who were justified in being in high positions were always asking themselves, "is it my brain or my ears that have put me in this position?" I am sure you can understand their feelings here. Getting rid of pinnarism in the way we had planned was making all micropinnates doubt their abilities.'

'I suppose every cat, no matter what size their ears, might have similar doubts', said Hamish. 'Am I in this position because I am worthy or am I just a pawn in the Pinnarism project?'

'All cats are equal, but we are not sure how equal', said Orwell.

Sagacity coughed. 'That's a good way of putting it. You've understood the problem very well. I think I can now give you some more information obtained by the Pinnarism Commission that I would prefer you to keep confidential. The Commission would not release them as they were so damning, but I can tell you there was a strong inverse relationship between the productivity of factories and other businesses and the cats in charge of them. Those run by small-eared cats were 30% less efficient than before. The same applied to degrees at the University. The pass rates were lower and the grades inferior to those in the past. Everyone said this was just a temporary blip following all the changes we had made but there was no evidence of improvement over time.'

'Does that mean that small-eared cats are simply not as good as those with large ears?' asked Hamish.

'No, you must not assume that – one of the reasons that the figures were not released is that many would make that assumption. We think, and are confident we are right, is that too many small-eared cats were catapulted into positions of responsibility before they were ready or perhaps should never have been promoted. So, when they all appeared on the cat walk nobody looked at the other parts of their bodies, their bearing or intellect by asking any pertinent questions; all attention was directed to their ears. They conquered all. Everything became completely lop-sided'.

Oscar laughed. 'My friend Samantha has got lop-sided ears. How would she be classified? As a unipinnate?'

'You may well laugh', said Sagacity, 'but defining these cats just became ludicrous. When a cat with unequal ears was being assessed they insisted on having a full family history extending back 100 years to determine their background. Good family from west Felixtown, out, poor family from East Felixtown, in. It was as stupid as that'.

'You mentioned learning at the beginning', said Hamish. 'How did that come in?'

'You have to thank your mentor, Professor Raggaty Doll, for that'. Sagacity clearly approved of him.

'Raggaty was asked to expose all the archives of the University so that all references to, and mention of, ears in the text, could be removed or replaced. He took a stand and refused to allow this to go ahead. The Otic Revolutionary Guard immediately sacked him. But Raggaty had anticipated this. All the other professors in the University resigned and stopped teaching. The students, who up until then were very much in favour of aggressive action against pinnarism, quickly realised that they would not be taught by experts and were very unhappy with the junior staff imposed on them by the Revolutionary Guard. So, after a stand-off of two months, Raggaty was reinstated and all the academic staff returned.'

'You said the last reason for the change was the growth of violence', said Hamish. 'Did that really affect the decision that led to all of us being released?'

'Yes, it was probably the most important reason, it turned the tide'. Sagacity was quite animated now. His marmalade fur was shining; he was in full orange mode.

'When the Commission looked at all the records of deaths and attacks since Wilberforce Shorthair started the Pinnarism Revolution they were quite shocked by the findings. Deaths due to attacks by large-eared cats on small-eared ones increased by 60 per cent in the first year – your brother, Torpedo, was sadly one of those statistics, and by 85% in the second, and with the growth of posotism the opposite reaction of small-eared cats assaulting big-eared ones increased three-fold in the two-year period. Nessie Wang at the hospital was very angry about it. 'Here we are, trying to promote mental health and increase the life span of cats', she said, 'and your policies are leading to the opposite. Cat lives are suffering, they are nasty, brutish and getting very short.'

But the real scandal was the finding that the Special Service of the Otic Revolutionary Guard was a killer group. Someone had the bright idea that if there were unexplained murders of micropinnates then it would promote the pinnarism project as it would keep cats on their paws and show how much reform was needed. Your brother, Torpedo, was killed by one of the cats in the squadron and as you were attacked afterwards by Groubadour we think he was the cat who had tried to kill you'.

Hamish was devastated by this admission.

'So, the Pinnarism project allowed killings to go on under its nose and did nothing about it?'

'Not exactly. Genghis Qualm set this up quite independently and after a little while it became secretive and isolated, and nobody knew what it was doing. But of course, once we knew all about this the Secret Service was disbanded immediately, Genghis was sacked as he should have kept a closer eye on what they were doing, and criminal enquiries followed. Many of the cats in the Secret Service were implicated and it was clear some of them were murderers.'

Of course, there was resistance to any change. The Otic Revolutionary Guard kept on insisting it was a temporary phenomenon and once they had got all cats under their control the death figures would fall. But they didn't and it was clear that the Guard were making everybody's lives much worse.

'That explains a lot. But what is going to be done now? You can't block out the pinnarism of the last few years as though it was never there.'

Sagacity was now getting really animated.

'Everything will depend of the vote on 22nd May. We would like to think most will vote in favour of the Pinnarism Agreement but it is far from sure as so many are invested in the present system.

'All the changes recommended by the Pinnarist Commission will lower the temperature of the debate. The big difference, if the Agreement is brought into law, is that cats can't just jump up and down shouting "pinnarism" whenever they are offended. Complaints are made in writing and until they are answered everything will remain private and confidential. So, all the silly suspensions and resignations that were preventing free speech should stop. Only serious instances of pinnarism will lead to retribution from the courts and these will set the tone of debate in a better way. But all depends on the vote'.

Hamish and Orwell thanked Sagacity for bringing them into his confidence. They knew it was really time to leave but their appetites had been so stimulated by the salmon and roe fritters they had to prolong the conversation just a little longer as they helped themselves to more. It had been a most revealing afternoon.

Epilogue - 23rd May, C1013

'It is another fine May morning here in Downcat Street. We are all waiting in anticipation for the results of the Pinnarism Agreement following the election yesterday. The result is expected imminently and we are waiting for the Prime Minister, Wilberforce Shorthair, to present it to the nation. Yes, he has finished licking himself and is about to give the results.'

Wilberforce came out and stood by the lectern. He cleared his throat

'The votes cast yesterday are as follows:

Yes, in favour of the Pinnarism Agreement, 69%

No, against the Pinnarism Agreement, 25%

Spoilt and scratched votes, 6%.'

The crowd in Downcat Street burst into applause. Wilberforce held up his hand; the applause subsided.

'The Pinnarism Agreement will now come into law. Thank you for your overwhelming support. We will continue to support the abolition of pinnarism but we have been overzealous in the past and have overstated its importance. We now have a softer and more compassionate way forward that prevents putting cat against cat and creating unnecessary conflict. I call upon you all to follow the agreement carefully, cautiously, but enthusiastically. I said three years ago that pinnarism had no place in our society. This belief remains; it is now for you to put it into effect'.

Applause ran out again as Wilberforce turned and returned to his home in 10 Downcat Street. His long-standing assistant, Larry, turned to the crowd and gently waved a paw before closing the door.

Acknowledgments:

I am grateful for the writings of Jonathan Swift, George Orwell, TS Eliot and John McWhorter in stimulating the development of this story. It was further crystallised by discussions with Patricia Casey, Swaran Singh, Peter Carter, Bryn Harris, and my daughter, Freya. Jennifer Barraclough also helped with her extensive knowledge of cat lore. My own cat, Hamish, was a constant support throughout. Steve Cawte has been with the project from the beginning and his constant support has been invaluable.

About the Author

Peter Tyrer wrote his first story about cats when he was 9 years old. The central figure was Cedric, a highly unreliable cat with a short attention span who was infuriatingly irritating and always getting into trouble. Since that time Peter has recognized that cats, when harnessed appropriately, can add a great deal to the happiness of humans and has developed this further by specializing in mental illness and supporting the introduction of pet therapy as a major treatment for mental illness. He has also realized that cats have far greater understanding of human problems than is commonly appreciated and thus explains the origin of this story. But all the cats in this tale would like to emphasise that this account is fictitious and that pinnarism is not present in cat society; it is only human frailty that has led feline society to place it there for educational purposes.

Printed in Great Britain
by Amazon

33085344R00089